SARAH

Joseph Miller is a proud man. When his daughter Sarah becomes personal maid to Lady Caroline, he resents her being a servant to the gentry. Worse still, her affair with the squire's son can only end in tragedy. Lady Caroline's wilful nature leads her into a clandestine romance with the estate bailiff, Thomas Cole. Selfishly and ruthlessly she carries gentle Thomas along on the tide of her passion. Nothing and no one must stand in her way, not even Lynwood, the young boy who loves her devotedly.

SARAH

SARAH

by

Margaret Dickinson

Magna Large Print Books
Long Preston, North Yorkshire,
England.

British Library Cataloguing in Publication Data.

Dickinson, Margaret
Sarah.

A catalogue record for this book is available from the British Library

ISBN 0-7505-0787-X

First published in Great Britain by Robert Hale Ltd., 1981

Published in Large Print January, 1996 by arrangement with Darley Anderson.

Magna Large Print is an imprint of
Library Magna Books Ltd.
Printed and bound in Great Britain by
T.J. Press (Padstow) Ltd., Cornwall, PL28 8RW.

CHAPTER 1

Abbeyford, England, 1795

'Smallpox!' Joseph Miller gaped at his wife, Ellen, in horror. 'Oh, no! *No!'*

He sank down on to the wooden chair at the side of the hearth. With her usual stoical acceptance of life's hardships, Ellen Miller continued to stir the gruel in the huge cooking-pot suspended from an iron crane over the fire.

'I was afeard of it when she fell ill three days back, but I kept it to mysel'.' She paused, then said flatly, 'Now I'm sure.'

'There's a rash?'

Ellen Miller nodded. 'All over 'er face, an' spreadin'.'

Joseph Miller groaned and dropped his head into his hands. 'Poor bairn. Poor Beth.' Then he raised his eyes and looked at his wife, his voice a hoarse whisper of fear. 'What of Sarah and little Ella?'

Ellen shrugged her shoulders, not because she did not care, but because there was nothing she could do.

'Time will tell,' she said sadly and began to ladle the hot liquid into a wooden bowl for her sick daughter.

'You've some red flannel?'

'Aye, an' I'll wrap her in it. But...' She left the words unsaid and moved towards the other room of their small cottage where her fifteen-year-old daughter lay shivering with a high fever.

Joseph hovered in the doorway for a moment watching the tortured twistings and delirious mumblings of his child. Then he turned away, helplessness bowing his strong shoulders.

He left the cottage to return to his work. There was still work to be done. No matter what affliction hit his family, there was always work to be done!

From his cottage Joseph Miller crossed the village green and took the path leading to the common land where the villagers grazed their own few livestock. A stream ran through the common land and beyond that, higher up the hill, stood the Manor House, a square, solid building with farm buildings behind it. Joseph Miller's face hardened. The Manor—and the Trents who lived there—ruled their lives. There was a deep-rooted bitterness in Joseph Miller's heart.

Hardship was no stranger to his family. Generations ago, under the open-field system, his forefathers had tilled their own strips of land, working only on the lord's land as payment of rent. But a Bill of Enclosure had changed all that. Now all the arable land, all the buildings, even the cottage which Joseph Miller called home, belonged to the Earl of Royston of Abbeyford Grange. And he preferred to let his land to one tenant farmer, Sir Matthew Trent, who in turn employed some of the villagers as his farm labourers. Now they worked the land that had once been their own for a weekly pittance. True, each villager had a strip of land behind his own cottage, but it was scarcely big enough to grow more than a few potatoes, support a few chickens or maybe a pig. They were becoming dependent upon the self-appointed 'squire', Sir Matthew Trent.

But a few—like Joseph Miller—still clung tenaciously to their self-sufficiency. They still had the right to graze their livestock on the common waste-land, and his wife, Ellen, and daughter, Beth, worked at the spinning-wheel to bring a little extra money into the home.

He stood a moment at the edge of the common watching his eldest daughter, black-haired, rosy-cheeked Sarah, tending their few sheep, two cows and ten geese. She wore a low-necked bodice, a coarse woven skirt hitched up to her knees and she had kicked off the clogs her father had made for her and ran barefoot.

'Sarah, oh Sarah,' Joseph Miller whispered in anguish. 'Not my pretty Sarah.' Stout-hearted though he was, the burly countryman felt a lump in his throat and tears prickle his eyelids at the mere thought of pretty, lively Sarah scarred to ugliness by smallpox—Sarah whom he could not help but love best of all of his three daughters.

For Beth he had a natural fondness and for little Ella an added feeling of protectiveness for she had not grown and developed as she should have done. Already Ella had brought Joseph and his wife sadness though through no fault of her own. She was a pretty ten-year-old with golden curls, but in her eyes there was a vacancy and a lack of understanding and when she did speak—which was rare—it was in the words of a five-year-old.

It was Sarah who brought Joseph joy, in whom he placed his trust and his hopes for the future. Her pertness enlivened his day, her willingness gladdened his heart and her beauty was his pride.

But now! What now?

'Come on, Pa,' she was calling to him with mock impatience as he neared her. 'It's time we wur milking. That un over there can 'ardly walk, her udder's that heavy.'

'Sarah,' he called, but already she was darting away from him, rounding up the straying cow. *'Sarah!* Come here, girl, I've something to tell you.'

'Aw, Pa!' She came reluctantly and he could feel her impatience to be off again.

'It's our Beth.'

'Beth? Is she worse?'

'Aye, I'm afeard so.'

'What—is it?' Now there was anxiety in Sarah's voice and her youthful restlessness was stilled by a chill of fear.

'Your ma says it's the smallpox.'

'Oh no!' Her violet eyes widened. Father and daughter stared at each other. At last Joseph Miller sighed and moved stiffly. 'Ah well, we've work to do, girl. While us can.'

'Aw Pa. Poor Beth.'

'Aye, poor Beth indeed,' he said bitterly and he glanced back over his shoulder towards the village. 'An' poor Abbeyford if it spreads among us all.'

Abbeyford nestled in its own shallow valley in rolling countryside some fifteen miles south of Manchester. Not that the cottagers knew much about life outside their own enclosed community. Most of them were born, grew up, fell in love, married, became parents themselves, grew old, died and were buried in the small churchyard in the centre of the village without ever having travelled more than a mile or two beyond the valley.

'Come on, let's get these cows milked,' Joseph said roughly to hide the growing terror in his heart.

Soberly now, with the carefree lightness gone from her step, young Sarah went about her work.

'You mun come an' stay with us, Sarah, out of harm's way.'

'I'll do no such thing, Henry Smithson,' Sarah snapped at the tall youth who stood over her, frowning heavily. Then regretful of her sharpness, for after all he was only thinking of her welfare, she said more gently, 'It's kind of you, but I mun stay with Ma and Beth and help where I can.'

'Aw Sarah, but if you should catch it...' Henry's eyes roamed over her clear skin, her rosy cheeks, her bright violet eyes and shining long black hair and the thought of her with that dreadful disease made him feel sick in the pit of his stomach.

'Sarah...?' His hand was on her arm. 'Let me speak to your Pa about us. I know you're young yet, but we could be promised.'

Sarah wriggled under his touch. She knew—it seemed as if she had always known—that Henry had a special feeling for her. Instinct had told her he was waiting for her to grow up. He wasn't exactly her cousin but their families were related way back.

Now he had put these feelings into words and Sarah wished that he had not. She had no desire to be tied by a promise at sixteen.

'Sarah—please...?'

'No, Henry. You know Pa wouldn't agree.'

The young man's frown deepened and

he said moodily, 'He'd agree if it wur what you wanted, Sarah.'

'Then you dunna know him as I do. Pa's got a right temper on him if things dunna go his way.'

Henry made a clicking noise of disbelief. 'Ach, you can twist him round your finger if you've a mind, Sarah.'

'That's where you're wrong, Henry,' Sarah replied quietly.

'Ah, an' it seems to me you're as stubborn as your Pa, an' all. All right, go home, go and catch the smallpox an' see if I care!'

Swinging his arms, Henry Smithson marched off up the lane towards his own home, his back rigid with anger. Despite his denial, the trouble was that he cared far too much for young Sarah!

Sighing, Sarah opened the door of the Millers' cottage, eager to see how her sister fared and yet reluctant to become involved in the atmosphere of sickness and worry. In the corner the spinning-wheel stood idle. Her mother was not in the one main room which served as kitchen-cum-living-room, but Sarah could hear sounds from the adjacent small room—her parents' sleeping quarters. Normally the three girls slept in the attic bedroom of the tiny cottage, directly under the thatch, but in times of sickness they were moved to their parents' room. Sarah stood in the doorway, almost recoiling from the sight of her poor sister.

Beth's face was blotched with small, hard pimples. For three days before the appearance of this rash she had been unwell with shivering fits and vomiting and had complained constantly of pains in her back and legs.

Now she lay quietly, her eyes closed as if sleeping.

'Ma?' Sarah whispered.

Ellen Miller turned. 'Don't come in here, Sarah.'

'But isn't there anything I can do to help?'

Ellen walked through to the kitchen, her movements slow and stiff as if she carried a great weight. She was a thin woman, slightly round-shouldered from the hours she spent at her spinning-wheel to augment the family income. Her hair, beneath her bonnet, was grey, her hands red and always a little swollen for there was never an idle day in Ellen Miller's life.

'Not for Beth—no,' she answered Sarah.

'But for yoursel'—keep away!'

'Ma, she's not...?'

'No, no, child. She's feeling better for the moment now the rash has come out.' Ellen glanced back towards the sickroom and sighed. 'But in a few days she'll be bad again when all those spots turn into abscesses. Here, help me tear this flannel into strips. It's an old remedy my own grandma told us—to wrap her in red flannel might stop her being so badly scarred.'

Silently Sarah tore the red material into strips.

'You know, Sarah, you could be safe from it.'

'Me? Why?'

'You had cowpox last year when you started helpin' milk up at the Manor.'

'So I did, but...'

'They reckon anyone who's had cowpox dunna get the smallpox.'

'Oh.' Sarah was thoughtful whilst she took in the full meaning for her. 'But Ella—she's not had the cowpox.'

'No, I know.'

'What about you an' Pa?'

'I reckon I had it as a child, but I dunna know about your Pa.'

'I hope it dunna spread round all the village,' Sarah murmured, but with little hope.

Beth's spots grew larger and became blebs of milky fluid; still growing, the fluid became a yellow pus and her face and body were covered with abscess-like spots. Round each tell-tale pock was an inflamed ring. The fever returned and Beth twisted and cried in pain, tearing the red flannel from her face and scratching in anguish at her swollen eyes.

Patiently Ellen nursed her daughter through the crisis. Her life was saved but not her smooth, childish complexion.

Beth's face was hideously marked with cruel pocks.

A little over two weeks after Beth, Ella fell ill too. Placid, docile Ella lay quite still, close to death and yet never a cry of complaint did she make. Meekly she submitted to being wrapped in red flannel and, when the worst was over, it was obvious that she was not to be so badly scarred as poor Beth who had repeatedly torn away the covering in her delirium.

As the Millers had feared the disease spread through the village, but no one else in their own family caught it.

Two babies, three older children and an elderly woman died and then came the shocking rumour—shocking to the villagers who believed that their own troubles and hardships never touched their betters.

Joseph brought home the news.

'Lady Caroline has the smallpox!'

Three pairs of eyes regarded him in surprise; Ella in her corner crooned softly to her rag-doll, lost in her own little world.

'Never!' exclaimed Ellen, whilst Beth fingered her own disfigured face.

'She'll not be so high 'n mighty if she ends up like me!' Since her illness, Beth's tongue had sharpened with bitterness.

Sarah was silent thinking of the girl she had seen so often in Lord Royston's open carriage around the lanes of Abbeyford. A pretty child. No, more than pretty, Sarah thought without envy. Lady Caroline was beautiful. Was that beauty to be lost for ever? Beth had not been what would be called pretty even before the smallpox. And now...

Sarah reached for her shawl from the hook.

'Where are you going, girl?' her father asked.

Sarah wrapped the shawl closely around her thin shoulders and lifted the latch on the door. 'To the Grange.'

'The Grange!' Her mother was scandalised. No villager ever approached Lord Royston's home without a very special reason. 'Whatever are you wantin' there, child?'

'I mun see how the li'le lady fares. Maybe there's summat as I can do to help.'

'Help! Help, is it?' Beth screamed, her blotched face growing purple. 'Who was there to help *me?*'

Sarah looked at her sister with pity, then without a word she turned and left the cottage.

Sarah crept along the edge of the gravelled driveway of Abbeyford Grange, not feeling quite so bold in her errand of mercy now she was in the shadow of the awesome building and the powerful gentry who lived there.

To her left stone steps led down into a sunken rose garden. She paused a moment to admire the profusion of pink roses. No other colour broke the mass of flaunting pink. Already the gardener was sweeping the fallen petals and cutting off the overblown blooms.

He looked up and stopped his sweeping. 'What you doin' here, young Sarah Miller?'

'I've come to see—to see...' she faltered and then took a deep breath and finished boldly, '...her ladyship about Lady Caroline.'

The gardener said soberly, 'The little maid has the disease.'

'I know—that's why I'm here.'

He resumed his brisk sweeping movements. 'It's an unhappy house. They'll not want to be troubled wi' likes of you.'

'We'll see,' Sarah said, confident that she would be heard if she brought hope for their beloved daughter.

Moments later she was facing the forbidding figure of the housekeeper at Abbeyford Grange. Mrs Hargreaves folded her hands neatly in front of her severe black dress and looked down upon the village girl who had presumed to present herself at the Grange.

'Well, and what do you want, girl?'

Though her knees trembled beneath her long skirt, Sarah said, 'I wish to see Lady Royston, if you please?'

The housekeeper's gasp of surprise was

plainly audible. 'Do you indeed? And what makes you so certain that her ladyship will condescend to see *you?*'

Sarah stuck out her chin defiantly. 'Because I've come to help her—to help Lady Caroline.'

Mrs Hargreaves gave a snort of contempt. 'If the best physicians in the county can do naught for the poor child, what can a chit like you hope to do, eh, miss? Tell me that?'

Sarah's clear violet eyes meet the cold gaze of the housekeeper unflinchingly.

'Besides,' Mrs Hargreaves continued, 'her ladyship is far too distraught to talk to *anyone,* let alone...'

'Then I'll speak to his lordship. I'm not afeard.'

'No, and more's the pity! A bit more respect for your betters, my girl, that's what...'

Sarah ignored the tirade of abuse and her sharp eyes spotted the staircase leading from the kitchens to the upper landings of the house. With the swift suddenness of youth, she dodged around Mrs Hargreaves and darted up the stairs before the housekeeper had realised what she was doing.

As the door swung to behind her, cutting off the indignant screech of the housekeeper, Sarah found herself in a vast, high hall, the staircase curving round and round, up and up. Ancestral paintings lined the walls, their cold, staring eyes reproving her bold entry into their world.

A young footman, hovering in the hall, almost dropped the tray he was carrying at the sudden arrival through the door of a village milkmaid.

At that moment the double doors leading to one of the rooms off the hall opened and Sarah found herself staring open-mouthed at the tall figure she knew to be Lord Royston. He, too, stopped in surprise to see her there, but there was neither the anger nor contempt on his face that she had seen in the expressions of the housekeeper and, even now, the footman.

She ran forward and bobbed a curtsy. 'Beggin' your pardon, m'lord,' she began breathlessly, 'but I heard Lady Caroline has the smallpox and I had to come, you see, perhaps I can help...'

At that moment a flustered Mrs Hargreaves arrived through the door and the footman too hurried forward and grasped Sarah roughly by the shoulder.

'I'm sorry, m'lord, I can't think how she got in...' he began, whilst behind them Mrs Hargreaves cried apologetically, 'Oh your lordship, I...'

Lord Royston raised his hand to quieten them both, his eyes upon the clear unwavering gaze of the girl standing before him. 'No—wait,' he said, his deep, soft tones instantly demanding respect and obedience. 'I wish to hear what this child has to say.'

'But, your lordship, she's naught but a village girl...'

Lord Royston's eyes burned fiery for a moment and the housekeeper fell silent.

'I will listen to anyone—*anyone*—who can perhaps help my daughter. Come, girl, come in and let me hear what it is you have to tell me.'

Standing in front of a blazing log fire with Lord Royston seated in front of her, Sarah explained.

'M'lord, my two sisters have had the smallpox an' me ma wrapped them both in red flannel, like her own grandma told her, to stop the scarring, m'lord.'

'And?' he questioned softly. 'Did it—help?'

'Well—Beth, she was that bad she tore off the binders and scratched at her face and, m'lord, she's terribly marked.'

'Poor child,' his lordship murmured, but Sarah knew his thoughts were more for his own daughter than for Beth Miller.

'But Ella, the youngest, she's a good li'le thing, she lay quiet and never moved the flannel me ma put on her.'

'And?' There was a note of pathetic eagerness in the earl's tone.

Sarah smiled. 'She's scarcely a mark on her, m'lord, not that won't fade given time, an' yet she had just as many spots as Beth at the start.'

'Red flannel, you say?'

'Yes, m'lord.'

He pondered a moment and then, with sudden decision jumped up and pulled violently on the bell-cord, shouting at the same time. 'Mrs Hargreaves—Mrs Hargreaves. Red flannel—have we any red flannel?'

Mrs Hargreaves appeared in the doorway. 'Why yes, m'lord. I believe so, but...'

'Wrap Lady Caroline in red flannel. See that her face is covered—particularly her face—but her hands and arms too. All must be wrapped in red flannel!'

'Yes, m'lord.' Mrs Hargreaves, peeved by her master's enthusiasm for this peasant girl's wild notion, nevertheless hurried to obey his orders.

More calmly, his lordship turned back to Sarah. 'And you—did not catch this dreadful disease?'

'No, m'lord. Me ma thinks it's because I caught the cowpox when I began working as milkmaid for Sir Matthew Trent. She's heard say as those as gets cowpox dunna get the smallpox.'

'Ah yes, yes. Indeed, I've heard of Mr Jenner who—now what do they call it?—vaccinates against this smallpox—and uses cows to do so. Ah, if only I had known in time, had thought...' Then he added, 'You're not afraid of catching the disease then?'

Sarah answered truthfully. 'At first I wur, m'lord. But now—well, I reckon if I wur goin' to get it I'd have it by now.'

'Yes, yes. Now listen, you have been a thoughtful girl to come here. Whether or not your idea works, I appreciate your concern for my daughter. Now—how would you like to become her personal maid, eh?' The earl even managed to smile, despite the heavy weight of anxiety he carried. 'She's been pestering me these last few months to allow her to have her own maid, just like her mother, instead of a governess.'

Sarah's mouth dropped open and she gaped in astonishment at Lord Royston. Never in her wildest daydreams could she have imagined herself, a lowly milkmaid, being offered such a position.

'Now, what do you say?' the earl prompted.

CHAPTER 2

'No, no, *no!*' Joseph Miller thumped the table with his clenched fist. 'She's not going up there. I won't have her going into service. She'll mix wi' bad company.'

Ellen Miller's spinning-wheel whirred all the faster. 'Joseph Miller, you're a good husband and father, I'll not deny, but do you want to see your daughter a milkmaid all her life? Dun't you want a better life for her? Why, at the Grange as Lady Caroline's personal maid, she's almost equal to Mrs Hargreaves. Just think—she's stepping straight into a good position, when most girls would start as kitchen-maid.'

'She'll still be a servant,' he muttered. 'We Millers call no one 'master'...'

Ellen sighed. She'd heard all this before.

'We hold our heads high, we're our own masters.' He thumped the table again. 'But between the pair o' them,' he gestured to one side of the valley towards Abbeyford Grange and then the other way towards the Manor. 'Between the two, they're trying to make lackeys out on us, on land we used to call our'n!'

'Joseph—it's better this way. The crops is better than when all the land was divided into strips. I remember me pa for ever complaining his land was ruined by couch-grass spreadin' from his neighbour's strip...'

'But it don't *belong* to us.'

'We still have the common land and...'

Joseph thumped the table again. 'Not for much longer it seems.'

Ellen's eyes widened and the rhythmic whirr of her spinning-wheel faltered. 'What do you mean?'

Joseph's voice became a low growl. 'Not content wi' robbin' us of our strips of arable land, they're going to enclose the common.'

'No!' Ellen gasped and the wheel stopped

completely. 'I dunna believe it.'

'Well, it's true. But this time they've a fight on their hands! We didn't fight last time because a lot o' the villagers thought Trent's arguments for increased production were sound. But we'll not let it happen *this* time!'

Ellen was silent. The arable land had been enclosed long before her marriage to Joseph, when they had been village children together, but she well remembered the anger of her own father and of Joseph's and the meetings they had held in their cottages to try to get all the villagers to unite against the Bill of Enclosure. But opinion had been varied. Some believed that they would be better off working for the Trents and the rebellion Joseph's father had tried to bring about had not happened.

Now she was to go through all that again.

They were silent for a moment, then his wife said tentatively, 'But you'll not stop Sarah going to the Grange, Joseph, will you?'

'I'd like to, but they'd turn us out of our home if I go agen them in every way. I reckon I dunna have no choice but to let her go,' he said bitterly, then added, clinging to a last, vain hope, 'Mebbe she'll not take to the life anyway.'

Sarah lay tossing and turning in the bed trying not to disturb her two younger sisters sleeping alongside her. She was far too excited for sleep! More than once she reared up on her elbows to look at the new grey dress and white lace cap and apron spread neatly over the box at the foot of the bed.

Tomorrow she was to begin working at Abbeyford Grange as Lady Caroline's personal maid. Of course, at sixteen—almost seventeen as she was quick to emphasise—it was not her first job. Since the age of nine she had worked in the fields gleaning after the harvesters; picking potatoes; bird-scaring; tending her father's livestock on the common land or driving them into the woods at the top of the hill. Then she had become a milkmaid at the Manor. But now...!

Sarah, in her shared bed, wriggled again.

'Go to sleep, our Sarah,' murmured Beth sleepily. But Sarah could not sleep. Tomorrow she would be up there with the gentry, part of their life-style. Never again would she have to suffer the backbreaking fieldwork, shed tears of pain over cold hands, chapped until they bled, or be driven half-mad by stinging chilblains, or risk being kicked by a stubborn cow. No longer for her, life in a farm-labourer's cottage.

From tomorrow onwards she would be sleeping in a soft feather-bed and have a room of her own. No longer would she bear the indignity of sharing a bed with her younger sisters.

Tomorrow she was to become a lady's-maid.

She was up before dawn, creeping across the cold floor of the attic bedroom in her bare feet to dress herself in the uniform of her new life, her fingers trembling with excitement.

She couldn't swallow any of the usual thick breakfast porridge and for a time she stood in the quiet confines of the small kitchen listening to the sounds of the cottage. She could hear her father snoring in the next room, the thrum of the wind in the chimney.

Sarah looked ruefully towards the almost cold grate of the kitchen fireplace. She ought to blow the fire back to life, but dressed now in her finery, her hands scrubbed to an unusual cleanliness, she refused to scrabble about with ashes and faggots.

She pulled her cloak around her and bit her lip with indecision. She was ready to go, anxious to be off, but knew she should say 'goodbye'. Not that she wouldn't be coming down to see them every week but her mother would never forgive her if she left without a proper farewell. Her pa, too, would want to warn her yet again to be a good girl and not to allow herself to be led astray.

She heard a movement in her parents' room and moments later her father appeared in the doorway, scratching his head and yawning. His bare feet stuck out below the shirt he wore day and night.

'Lord! You up already, me girl?'

'Yes, Pa. I couldna sleep.'

He yawned again and grinned at her. 'You're lucky! I reckon I could sleep for a hundred years and then some.' He paused and his eyes roved proudly over her heart-shaped face with its smooth rosy skin, the pert nose and generous mouth. Her violet eyes were shining with excitement and her cascading unruly black hair was gathered neatly now beneath the white lace cap. Then, as he noticed her new finery, his smile faded. 'You're off then?' he said gruffly.

'Aw Pa, dun't spoil it for me.'

He sat down on the hard chair and began to pull on his working boots. 'You'd do better to settle down and marry Henry.'

'I dunna want to marry Henry, Pa, nor anyone else. Not yet.'

He wagged his finger at her. 'Don't you go gettin' fancy ideas about yoursel', me girl.'

'No, Pa. I'll work hard—and I'll be good,' she added impishly.

'Aw,' Joseph Miller doubled his fist and landed a gentle mock blow upon her chin, but now he was smiling. 'Go on wi' you! You'd best say 'goodbye' to your ma,' he jerked his thumb towards the next room, 'then you can be off.'

As she pulled the cottage door shut behind her, Sarah breathed deeply in the fresh morning air. Directly in front of her was the village green with its duck-pond and on the far side the vicarage and the church and churchyard.

She turned left and walked along the

lane, past the line of cottages which bordered the green. The lane curved to the right and then swung sharply left away from the green. More cottages lined the road on either side now and amongst them on the right-hand side was the village's one inn, the Monk's Arms. Sarah walked on, the road curving left towards the bridge over the stream. The last two buildings of the village, close beside the stone bridge, belonged to the smith and his brother, the village wheelwright. Already she could hear the clanging sounds of the smith's heavy hammer. Beyond the bridge the trees overhung the lane, almost touching at the top and forming a shadowy, natural tunnel.

Sarah took another deep breath and gave a little skip of sheer delight. More sedately, as befitting her new position, she walked on, climbing the hill on the eastern side of the valley towards Abbeyford Grange standing proudly just below the summit of the hill, sheltered from the cold easterly winds.

She paused at the huge wrought-iron gates leading into the grounds of the Grange and gazed in awe at the black and white mansion, with four gables at the front and one over the porch entrance. The house was built of wood and plaister, reminiscent of the Tudor age, but had been built in the early part of the seventeenth century by the first Earl of Royston.

Sarah turned to look back down into the valley. Her own home looked minute now, almost lost to the eye amongst the row of cottages nestling around the village green.

Directly opposite the Grange about halfway up the western hill stood Abbeyford Manor. It was a square, solid house with stables to one side and farm buildings at the rear, and had been built by the fourth Earl of Royston for his younger son and his bride and completed in 1741, but the young couple had died without heirs. Then, after the Bill of Enclosure, the house had become the home of the Earl's tenant farmer. To young Sarah the Manor was a fine house, but nothing like as grand as Abbeyford Grange.

Robert Elcombe, the sixth Earl of Royston, owned Abbeyford Grange and all the surrounding farmland and woodland upwards of a thousand acres. He owned all the cottages in the village, even the vicarage and the Monk's Arms. His tenant farmer, Sir Matthew Trent, who occupied

Abbeyford Manor, now farmed the land, though the earl himself took an active interest in the running of the estate and employed a forester and a gamekeeper to tend the woodland, the game-birds and trout-streams. Only the common waste-land belonged by feudal right to the cottagers—and now it seemed even that was to be taken from them.

But Sarah was not worrying about such things on this most important day. Her mouth curved in a small smile as she surveyed the valley beneath her, her eyes fondly following the twisting paths of the streams, one which ran down the hillside on which she stood, the other running from the north-west corner of the valley and through the common. The lane leading from the village up to the Manor ran through this stream, literally, for there was only a narrow footbridge across the water at this point. Farm carts, or the gentry's carriages, had to splash through the ford in the lane, which in times of heavy rain could become treacherously deep. At the southern end of the valley the two streams joined together and ran as one out of the valley through a natural pass between the hills to join a river some miles away.

Above the Manor and a little to the south, gaunt and black against the skyline stood the abbey ruins on the very top of the hill. Sarah's gaze finished its roving and with a last glance towards the tiny cottage she called home—as if to draw courage from it—she turned her back upon the valley and entered the gates of Abbeyford Grange.

'So you are to be Lady Caroline's personal maid, Sarah Miller?' Mrs Hargreaves, the housekeeper, stood before her.

'Yes'm,' Sarah whispered. Mrs Hargreaves's hair was stretched tightly back from her face beneath a white muslin cap with a ruffled frill. Her cold grey eyes bulged slightly and beneath her small mouth her chin sloped sharply inwards so that her overlarge nose dominated the whole of her face. She launched into a seemingly endless list of a personal maid's duties, most of which flowed directly over Sarah's head. The night's excited anticipation was giving way to dread now.

'...And finally, you will be allowed one half-day off a week and every fourth Sunday.' The housekeeper paused and looked keenly into Sarah's pert face. 'Servants are not allowed followers. Do you know what that means?'

'Yes'm.'

'And don't get above yourself, just because his lordship thinks your idea worked for Lady Caroline. He can't see that it was just a way of trying to better yourself.' Mrs Hargreaves thrust her sharp features close to Sarah's face with undisguised malevolence. 'It didn't help poor Lady Royston did it, Miss Clever? You're nothing more than a cowgirl and never will be!'

She straightened and sniffed contemptuously. 'But there's no dissuading his lordship. You're here, so you'd better follow me and I'll take you to Lady Caroline.'

It was two months since Sarah had come boldly to Abbeyford Grange. Lady Caroline had recovered from the smallpox and, to Lord Royston's mind thanks to Sarah Miller, would be very little scarred. But three weeks after Caroline had first become ill, her mother, Lady Royston, had contracted the smallpox and, despite the attendance of three physicians and the further use of red flannel, on the ninth day of her illness Lady Adeline Royston had died.

Meekly Sarah followed the housekeeper up the back stairs and through a door on the first floor landing which divided the servants quarters from the rest of the house. Silently now on the thick carpet they walked along the gallery overlooking the main staircase. Heavy chandeliers hung from the ceiling and tapestries lined the walls. In the north wing of the house Mrs Hargreaves paused, rapped sharply on a door and when she was bade, 'Come in,' opened the door and ushered Sarah into the most beautiful bedroom the girl had ever seen.

Sarah Miller, born and raised in a cottage, had never imagined such luxury even existed. The white plaster ceiling was embossed with figures of cherubs playing various musical instruments, the pink-flowered wallpaper complemented the pale pink flower-sprigged silk of the bed canopy and drapes. The fireplace was marble with embossed decoration, picked out again in pink. The chairs and dressing-stool were upholstered in pink silk brocade and the whole effect was utterly feminine and luxurious.

'This is Sarah Miller, Lady Caroline. Your—er—personal maid.'

The young woman sat up in bed, yawned, stretched and smiled a little wanly at Sarah. 'Thank you, Mrs Hargreaves, that will be all.'

'I have explained her duties to her, and...'

'Yes, yes,' Lady Caroline said a little impatiently.

'Lady Caroline,' Mrs Hargreaves said stiffly and, as the door closed behind the rigid figure of the housekeeper, Lady Caroline held out her hands towards Sarah.

'I'm so glad you're here,' she told the surprised girl. Closer now, Sarah could see for herself that, though at present Caroline's skin was not as clear and smooth as it had once been, the pock-marks were such that would soon fade and she would bear only one or two scars—easily disguised—on her lovely face.

'This is the first time I've been allowed a maid of my very own,' Lady Caroline was saying, stretching and running her fingers through her tumbling auburn hair. 'Until now my life has been ruled by nannies or governesses. Of course, my mother...' Her voice broke a little for the loss of her mother was still very new and painful. '...always had her own maid. Do you know it has taken me a whole *year* to persuade Papa to allow me a maid of my very own?'

Sarah smiled. Lady Caroline was only a year or so older than Sarah herself and she was relieved that her attitude towards her maid was, though perhaps a little unconventional, more friendly than Sarah had expected. It helped to lessen the hostility in the housekeeper's eyes.

'Well—you might as well start right away. Did Mrs Hargreaves show you your room?'

'No, m'lady. She b-brought me straight up here.'

'Never mind,' Caroline waved her hand airily. 'Take off your cloak and put it over there.'

As she did so, Sarah listened to Lady Caroline's instructions. 'I take a bath every morning at eight o'clock. The housemaids bring up the water, but you should be here to see that everything is prepared just as I like it, and all my garments ready for the day. I usually go riding most mornings before I have breakfast at nine-thirty, but recently, since my illness, I've risen later. Papa thinks I am well enough to go out a little now and this afternoon I shall drive over to Lynwood Hall. Lady Lynwood is—was—a dear friend of Mama's and—and I should like to see her.' There was a wistfulness in the girl's voice. Then, with a determined effort to be more cheerful, she added, 'And you shall come with me. After all, you'll be replacing old Ropey as my companion.'

'Who—who was old Ropey?' Sarah dared to ask.

'Miss Roper—my governess.' Caroline sat down on the silk-covered stool before the dressing-table, picked up a hairbrush and began to brush the tangles from her long hair. 'Here, you should be doing this now.'

Sarah took the brush her mistress held out to her and with trembling fingers began to brush Lady Caroline's hair with tentative strokes.

'Harder, Sarah, harder. It must be smooth and shining. One hundred strokes a day, old Ropey used to say.'

Sarah obeyed.

'That's better,' Lady Caroline murmured and with her first words of praise Sarah's confidence began to grow.

That afternoon Sarah found herself seated in the gig, bowling along the country lanes, the reins in the confident, expert hands of Lady Caroline. As they neared the ford in the road, Sarah's tongue ran round her lips fearfully and she found her hands gripping the side of the vehicle. But Lady Caroline merely gave a sharp slap of the reins, the horse quickened pace and they splashed through the water safely. Then they were climbing the hill.

'That's the road leading to the Manor.' As they reached a fork in the lane, Lady Caroline pointed to the left. 'But we take the right-hand road to Amberly and then on to Lynwood Hall.' They reached the top of the hill and passed beneath the trees of the wood. 'Have you been this way before, Sarah?'

'Only to Amberly, m'lady. I walked it once with Henry.'

'Who—is Henry?'

Remembering Mrs Hargreaves's warning against 'followers' Sarah imagined Lady Caroline's question to hold an ominous note. Swiftly she assured her, 'Oh, he's only a distant cousin, m'lady.'

Beyond the wood they left the boundary

of Lord Royston's lands and entered the Lynwood estate. They passed through the village of Amberly. On either side now Sarah saw fields of waving, golden corn. In one field she could see a line of reapers rhythmically swinging their sickles as they moved slowly forward, the corn falling with each cut. Then other men were loading it on to a wagon, pulled by four huge shire-horses, their harness glinting in the sunlight. Several children followed the reapers and Sarah allowed herself a small smile of satisfaction to think that she was riding beside her mistress instead of bent double in the cornfield.

Skilfully Lady Caroline turned the gig through the gates leading to the parkland of Lynwood Hall and they followed the winding driveway leading to the house itself. Deer, grazing in the meadows on either side, raised their heads to watch the gig rattle past.

Ahead of them Sarah could now see a vast, square mansion of three storeys, the ground floor being set halfway below ground level. A straight balustrade of pinnacles surrounded the flat roof. The smooth lawn before the main entrance was completely encircled by the driveway and, to the side of the house, the ornamental gardens led down to a lake where swans swam upon the water, their white plumage shining in the sun. Fountains played in the gardens, the shimmering water cascading like silver.

'It's even bigger than Abbeyford Grange,' Sarah said, forgetting her shyness in her wonder.

Lady Caroline laughed, for the moment her recent suffering and bereavement banished from her mind. 'Don't let my Papa hear you compare Abbeyford Grange unfavourably with Lynwood Hall. He and Lord Lynwood used to argue constantly about the relative merits of their estates and houses. But they were the best of friends really,' she added, jumping down from the gig as they came to a halt outside the main steps of the Hall. Awkwardly, unused to riding in such a grand manner, Sarah climbed down and followed her mistress.

They were shown into Lady Lynwood's small sitting-room, Sarah hovering uncertainly in her mistress's wake.

Briefly, with a wave of her hand, Lady Caroline dismissed her. 'Sarah, go with the footman. He'll take you somewhere you can wait until I'm ready to leave.'

'Yes, m'lady.' As she turned to follow the liveried footman, Sarah saw Lady Lynwood rise and move forward to greet Caroline.

'My dear Caroline, how wonderful to see you well again!' Lady Lynwood was a handsome woman, with bright, merry eyes and black hair with a single streak of white rising from the centre of her brow and sweeping over the crown of her head. Her figure was still slim and surprisingly youthful. As Sarah followed the footman, she passed a young boy of about fourteen hurrying to enter the room she had just left. He was a good-looking, fair-haired boy, but he spared not a glance for Sarah.

'Who was that?' she whispered to the footman.

'That was Francis Amberly, Lord Lynwood. He's a bit partial to Lady Caroline. Very forward for his age, is young Francis!'

'Is he a 'lord'? He dun't seem old enough for a title.'

'Young Francis succeeded to the title three years ago when his father died. Age has nothing to do with it.' The footman laughed derisively. 'You don't know much about the nobility, do you, miss?'

Sarah coloured and said, hotly defensive, 'I am Lady Caroline's personal maid.'

The footman bowed towards her mockingly. 'Pleased to make your acquaintance, ma'am!'

He opened the door leading to the servants' domain and they clattered down the stairs, the warmth and noise from the busy kitchens rushing up to envelop them.

'Here's my Lady Caroline's personal maid come to honour us with a visit,' he announced as he ushered her into the main kitchen. Three pairs of eyes were turned upon her, but the work did not pause for an instant. The cook continued to beat batter in a large bowl, the kitchen-maid continued to chop vegetables and the housemaid's duster never faltered over the spoon she was polishing so vigorously.

'Come away in, my dear,' the cook smiled kindly. 'Take no notice of young William, he's a big tease, ain't he, Martha?'

The housemaid nodded ready agreement. 'A sight too ready with his tongue, if you ask me.' And she cast a withering glance towards the young footman, but he only laughed, bowed mockingly once more but this time to include all of them and left.

'Sit you down, me dear. What's your name?' the cook continued, still slapping at the batter in her bowl with uninterrupted rhythm.

'Sarah. Sarah Miller.'

'You been with Lady Caroline long?'

'This is my first day.'

'Is it now?'

'Yes. To tell you the truth,' she felt the urge to confide in the friendly cook, 'it's all a bit strange.'

'Ah well—you'll soon settle in. We've all got to start somewhere.' She nodded her head towards the silent kitchen-maid. 'I started as a kitchen-maid, like young Annie here. You think yoursel' lucky to have got a job as personal maid already. How old are you?'

'Seventeen. Well—nearly.'

'There you are then! Lucky, you are. Annie's a year older 'n you and still a kitchen-maid. A bit slow, she is, but she's willin', aren't you, Annie?'

The girl nodded and smiled, not in the least insulted.

'You work hard and you'll go up in the world, young Sarah, mark my words. And Lady Caroline—she's a lovely girl. Ah, but we was that sorry to hear poor Lady Royston had gone. As I tell Annie here, mebbe we sometimes envy the folks we works for, but for all their riches it don't stop 'em havin' troubles sometimes just like the rest of us, do it now? But you're lucky, an' no mistake, young Sarah.'

Yes, thought Sarah, she was lucky, very lucky, but she couldn't help wishing that this kindly body was in charge of the staff at Abbeyford Grange instead of the sour-faced Mrs Hargreaves.

The days passed into weeks and the weeks into months and, once the period of mourning was over for Lady Royston, Sarah began to find out what it was really like to be a 'lady's-maid'. Even when, on her days off, she visited her family, she could hardly wait to climb the hill once more back to Abbeyford Grange.

Her mother revelled in her good fortune, but Joseph Miller said little. Henry would tease her about her lofty position.

'I mun doff my cap when I speak to you soon, young Sarah.'

At first his teasing was good-humoured, but gradually, as her family were subjected on her every visit to her ceaseless recounting of what Lady Caroline said or did, how things were done at the Grange and how her mistress depended upon her so, Henry's words began to take on an unfortunate ring of truth.

'You're getting above yoursel', young Sarah,' he told her soberly as he walked her up the lane in the dusk of evening on her return to Abbeyford Grange after a visit home.

Sarah tossed her head. 'I'm sure I don't know what you mean, Henry.'

'Look,' he stopped and took her by the shoulders forcing her to stop and turn to face him. 'It's time we got things straight 'atween us. You're seventeen now and I want to speak to your pa about us.'

'About us? What d'you mean?' She pretended not to understand him.

He gave her shoulders a little shake. 'You know very well, Sarah. Don't play fancy games wi' me. It's time there was an understanding 'atween us. You know I want to marry you...'

Sarah's eyes widened and she blurted out. 'They don't allow no followers, Henry. You know that.'

He gave a little click of exasperation. 'They needn't know. They've never said anything about me seeing you back at night on your days off, have they?'

'No,' Sarah said doubtfully, 'but...'

'Well then, they wun't know no more than that. Come on, Sarah, what about it?'

Sarah wriggled to escape his grasp. 'I'll think about it, Henry. I'm fond of you, you know that, but...'

'But what?' His face darkened with hurt pride. 'Not good enough now, aren't I? For Lady Caroline's lady's-maid!'

Sarah was silent. She could not deny that since living at the Grange she had begun to notice the vast difference between her own background and that of Lady Caroline's upbringing.

Sarah's own rough edges were automatically being smoothed by her new environment, so much so that her family's coarse manners, rough ways and poor circumstances grew daily more apparent—and more abhorrent—to her.

'Don't despise your own folk, Sarah,' Henry said as a parting shot as he swung open the wrought-iron gate for her to pass through into the grounds of the Grange. ' "Pride goeth 'afore a fall" as Parson's allis tellin' us,' he added darkly and swung the gate shut with a heavy clang.

He stood watching her walk up the drive realising that not only the ironwork of the gate physically between them separated their two lives now.

CHAPTER 3

Sir Matthew Trent leaned back in his leather chair, and, fingertips to fingertips, eyed the red-faced Joseph Miller standing before him.

The difference between them was marked. The 'master' was elegantly dressed in tight-fitting pantaloons, a striped silk waistcoat over which he wore a tailed coat. A silk cravat nestled against his throat and his own hair, still a rich red colour with scarcely a speck of grey, was worn long and tied at the nape of his neck.

In contrast Joseph Miller wore rough knee-breeches, a loose, open-necked shirt and stout, home-made boots. His wiry hair, once black, was now completely grey; his face was weather-beaten and lined by the years of hard work. Whilst the master's hands were pale and smooth with a signet-ring on his fourth finger, Joseph Miller's hands were gnarled and dirty.

But he stood before Sir Matthew with no feeling of inferiority. Joseph Miller was a proud man, despising Sir Matthew for the way he made his living—by the labour of others.

'You've already taken away the land we cultivated, now you're trying to take away our grazing rights on the common waste.'

'Not quite, Miller, not quite. The wastes must be enclosed. Each man must pay his share of the legal expenses and enclose his own allotment with fences or hedges and ditches.'

'Not one of us villagers could afford to do that,' Joseph Miller growled.

Sir Matthew shrugged his shoulders and spread his hands, palms upwards. 'That is hardly my concern. Lord Royston is willing to buy out any man who cannot afford to do the necessary...'

'You know well enough there's not one amongst us who can,' Joseph Miller stormed. 'It's just a way to get ownership of *all* the land around here, to say nothing of our homes.'

'The war with France has compelled

us to increase food production—quickly. Now, be reasonable. This area is excellent for cattle-rearing and I propose to increase the size of my herd considerably. What do you say to becoming my head cowman, Miller?'

'Bribery, is it?' Joseph Miller thundered, forgetting the need for caution. 'You take away my livelihood with one hand and offer me work with the other.'

'So? I fail to see what is so wrong with that.' Sir Matthew, with a supreme effort, retained his patience. ' 'Tis nothing to be ashamed of to be a good, honest working man.'

'What of those men who lose their grazing rights and yet have no work? I canna see you being able to employ all the menfolk of the village.'

'Perhaps not, but there is work a-plenty in the cities. The textile trade in Lancashire is undergoing a vast change. Exciting changes, my man...'

'These are country-bred folk an' want naught to do wi' cities and manufactories.'

'Well then, I'm sorry,' Sir Matthew said curtly, his pale blue eyes hard and cold. 'There's work to be had if they're enterprising enough. But as for the enclosure of the common land—it will become law very soon and there's nothing you nor I—nor anyone else—can do about it.'

'Nor do you want to, I'm thinkin',' Joseph Miller muttered.

Sir Matthew was on his feet, the anger he had purposely held in check overflowing. 'I'll see you get no work hereabouts, Miller. I'll not have trouble-makers amongst my employees.'

'I'd sooner starve first!'

The two men glared at each other and Sir Matthew said tightly, 'Your attitude may well bring you to it, Miller. It may well bring you to it!'

Once more, as his father had before him, Joseph Miller found himself without allies against the enclosure of the common land.

'But 'ee pays good wages, Joseph,' Seth Brindley argued. 'Better'n some as I've 'eard tell.'

'That's only to get you into his employment, to get you entirely dependent on him. Then what? We'd be no better than those black slaves they bring into Liverpool by the boatload!'

'Well....' Seth cast about for some

reasoned argument. He liked working for Sir Matthew, knowing that at the end of each week he would have a regular income. The uncertainty of grubbing his own living from meagre strips of land and his own scrawny three or four cows had been replaced by a comforting sense of security. 'Well, 'ee seems fair to me,' he ended lamely. ' 'Ee gave me a good price for me cattle.'

Joseph brought his fist down upon the scrubbed table. 'Mebbe so—now. An' to those whom he offers employment.' Joseph leaned towards Seth, who backed away. 'What of all those who he don't employ? What's to become of them?'

Seth was silent. He had not the intelligence nor the foresight of Joseph Miller. Amongst the simple country folk, Joseph Miller was something of an individual. Though, like them, he could neither read nor write, his intelligence and logical reasoning far outstripped that of the ordinary labouring man.

Seth—and all his kind—lived for today, but Joseph Miller could visualise tomorrow —and he did not like what he saw!

Autumn gave way to winter and with the

harvest over the villagers began to plan for their Christmas celebrations. Every year Sir Matthew held a festive gathering in his huge barn at the back of the Manor for all the villagers—an event anticipated with pleasure by everyone. Even Joseph Miller would put aside his resentment and join the merry-making.

Lady Caroline said, 'Sarah, I shall join the villagers' celebrations this year.'

Sarah looked up, her action in folding Caroline's undergarments stilled. 'Will your Papa allow it, m'lady?' the young girl asked doubtfully. Though Lord Royston doted on his vivacious daughter and spoilt her in many ways, lavishing gifts on her and arranging the life of the Grange around her, Sarah could not believe that he would allow Caroline to mix socially with the workers on his estate.

Lady Caroline shrugged her smooth shoulders and thought for a moment. 'I'll ask Guy Trent to escort me.'

Sarah thought about the wild young man she frequently saw galloping about the district on his horse, usually at a distance. But only the previous week he had spoken to her for the first time. She had been walking home down the lane from the

Grange on her free afternoon when the sound of thudding hooves behind her had made her scurry to the side of the road. Guy Trent had pulled his temperamental chestnut stallion to a standstill, whilst he grinned down at Sarah, who drew further back on to the grass verge away from the restless animal's pawing hooves.

'Good-day, Miss Miller.'

Sarah gave a startled gasp, surprised that he should know her name. Then, as if reading her thoughts, he laughed, showing white, even teeth. His red hair was fashionably long and tied at the nape of his neck, but he spurned the wearing of a hat. His blue eyes had twinkled roguishly down at her. He was short and stockily built, but for a man who led the life of an idle gentleman his shoulders were broad and his muscles powerfully developed. She had heard he joined in with the village youths—wrestling, bare-knuckle fighting and other such contests of strength.

'Don't look so frightened. What have they told you about me, eh Sarah? Have they told you what a wicked fellow I am?'

Sarah had taken another step backwards.

'Yes—I mean, no, sir.'

Guy's laughter had rung out, then his expression had softened. He had steered his mount close to her, reached down and touched her cheek with the tips of his fingers. 'Don't be afraid of me, Sarah, I wouldn't want to hurt a pretty little thing like you.'

His touch had seemed to burn her cheek and, with a swift intake of breath, she had leapt back yet again. 'I mun go,' she had muttered and turned to hurry on down the lane, her heart beating alarmingly.

'I'll see you again, lovely Sarah,' he had called after her and seconds later she was obliged to step again into the grass at the side of the lane as he galloped past, the panting horse's thudding hooves so close.

As she emerged from the shade of the overhanging trees, at a bend in the road she had seen him leap a hedge into a field and gallop wildly down the steep-sloping meadow towards the stream. Madly he had plunged his mount into the water, splashed through the stream and climbed up the opposite bank. He had pulled on the reins, bringing his horse to a standstill. Then he had swung round and waved to her again.

'We'll meet again, Sarah,' he had shouted, his words reaching her faintly on the breeze. She had looked about her anxiously, afraid that someone would hear his wild promise.

When she had looked back at Guy Trent, he was galloping across the common, through the herd of cows grazing there and across the second stream and up the opposite hill towards the Manor.

Remembering her meeting with him brought a faint blush to her cheeks as she recalled too the rumours she had heard about Guy Trent concerning two or three village girls; the warning her father had given her so many times, 'You keep away from Master Guy, our Sarah. He's a wild one and no mistake. Don't let him charm you wi' his fancy talk. He's a rogue.'

In the next breath Lady Caroline herself confirmed this. 'He's a philanderer, of course, but,' she sighed, 'since I am to be stuck here in the country until the next London season, he's the nearest there is to a suitable escort. And Sir Matthew and Lady Penelope will be there, so perhaps Papa won't object.'

At first Lord Royston did object, but

Caroline wheedled and coaxed until he relented.

If only he could have foreseen the disastrous consequences which were to follow this one, seemingly innocuous, merry-making event, he would have locked his precious daughter in her pink room and thrown away the key!

Sarah arrived at the barn with her own family. She was wearing the finest dress she had ever possessed—a discarded gown of Caroline's altered to fit the smaller, thinner Sarah. It was a full-skirted pale pink gown with a pleated flounce at the hem and also on the sleeves. The neckline was low with a black velvet bow at the bosom.

Henry Smithson was both admiring and yet suspicious. 'You look the right lady now,' he said, an edge of sarcasm to his tone.

Sarah laughed and her eyes sparkled, intoxicated by the excitement and the atmosphere. The barn was lit by numerous rush-lights and warmed by the earthy smell of the animals who normally wintered there.

'Come on, Henry, let's dance,' Sarah begged, eager to join the red-faced sweating villagers jigging about to the surprisingly tuneful noise issuing forth from the motley selection of instruments which the villagers always managed to produce on these occasions.

Reluctantly he allowed himself to be dragged into the mêlée of the boisterous villagers. Whilst Sarah was light on her feet, a natural dancer, Henry was clumsy, growing red with embarrassment at every faltering step.

'Aw, I ain't no good at this, our Sarah,' he puffed, but Sarah merely laughed and continued to skip lightly around him on her toes. Out of the corner of her eye she saw Lady Caroline dancing with Guy Trent and envy flooded through her. They made such a handsome couple, dancing so expertly together that they outshone everyone else.

Lady Caroline's entrance a few moments earlier on Guy's arm had surprised and confused the villagers. They were a little shy of continuing their celebrations in her presence. Guy Trent's arrival did not disturb them, for he was frequently in the company of the young men of the village—and of the young girls too, much to their parents' chagrin! They were all used to the Trents' attendance, but not that of Lord Royston or his daughter. But when they realised that she meant to join in their festivities whole-heartedly, they forgot their shyness and the chasm between their social positions. When the spiced ale had inspired confidence, they ceased to be embarrassed.

Whilst Sarah danced with the clumsy Henry, casting envious glances at her young mistress, Guy Trent led Caroline towards the corner of the barn where his particular friends had gathered.

'No bad language, you fellows,' Guy laughed as he presented Caroline to them. 'We have a *lady* amongst us.'

Caroline shot him a look of annoyance. She did not want to be marked out as someone different. Tonight she wanted to be one of them. She smiled brightly at the four faces before her, all of whom she knew by sight.

There was Joe Robinson, the village smith; Will Briggs, the son of the landlord of the Monk's Arms; Patrick O'Reilly, the forester on the estate, and Thomas Cole, the estate's bailiff and Abbeyford's parish constable. They all rose and greeted her pleasantly and Thomas Cole offered her his place on a bale of hay.

'Thank you.' She bestowed upon him her most brilliant smile and the quiet Thomas Cole, shy of women, was utterly captivated. He was scarcely taller than Caroline with soft, wavy brown hair and a skin tanned to a pale bronze from being out riding around the estate on his horse in all seasons. He was not a conventionally handsome man, but his face mirrored the kindness and gentleness that was his nature and his smile made deep furrowed creases in his cheeks and around his eyes.

'What a noise!' Caroline laughed and leant towards him. 'But they seem to be enjoying themselves enormously.'

Thomas Cole's shyness intrigued Caroline. The young men of her acquaintance, of the same social standing as herself, dandies all, were over-confident, superior beings, treating her with an air of charming condescension. Now this quiet, thoughtful man was looking at her with such admiration in his tender eyes that it made her girlish heart turn over. And despite his air of diffidence there was an earthy strength and virility about him that excited her as no other man had ever done.

'I've seen you riding about the estate,' she told him, herself feeling an unaccustomed self-consciousness under his steady, bemused gaze. For some reason she could not herself explain, Caroline wanted this man to think well of her.

She need not have worried. Thomas Cole could hardly believe his good fortune to be here talking to this lovely creature, the goddess he had only ever seen before from a remote distance.

'Yes, m'lady.'

'Oh please call me Caroline—for tonight at least,' she added swiftly, lest her bold suggestion that they forgo formality would offend his idea of propriety. She patted an empty place at the side of her. 'Please tell me about yourself,' she asked, Guy Trent quite forgotten as Thomas Cole sat down beside her.

The smile creased his face and Caroline found herself smiling in response—that was what his smile did to people. They just had to smile in return and Lady Caroline at this moment was the very last person to wish to fight against the natural instinct.

'There's not much to tell, really,' Thomas Cole began, in his soft, deep voice, and for something to occupy his nervous hands he fished out his pipe from his pocket and began to fill it. Fascinated, Caroline watched his strong fingers packing the brown tobacco into the bowl of the pipe shaped in a fox's head.

'I've never seen a pipe like that before.'

He held it out towards her and she took it from him and held it, cradling it in her soft hands. The tangy smell of the tobacco rose to her nostrils, but it was the intricate, perfect carving of the fox's head which intrigued her.

'It's beautiful,' she murmured and handed it back to him. As he took it their fingers brushed, the merest touch like a butterfly's wings, but it was enough to make their eyes meet each other's steadfast gaze and to feel the tingling run from the touching fingers through the whole of their bodies.

Thomas was the first to break the spell, as if realising suddenly that he had no right to look at the earl's daughter in such a way. Just because she had come amongst them at Christmas to join in their festivities was no reason to suppose that the closeness could continue once Christmas was over.

But Caroline was feeling acute disappointment as he cleared his throat and looked away from her.

'I was born in Amberly,' he was saying. 'My father was bailiff on the Lynwood estate and I began work under him.'

'You said *was* Lynwood's bailiff?' she prompted softly.

'He died last year.'

'I'm sorry,' and her tone held genuine sympathy, not merely the utterance of obligatory condolence. 'You didn't take over in his place then?'

'No. I was already employed here and well settled. And there was no reason to move back. My mother had died two months before him.'

'Oh how dreadful for you!' Caroline said. 'To lose both of them in such a short space of time.'

She glanced down at her hands lying in her lap. The pain of her own loss was still fresh. She raised her green eyes to look into his gentle ones. 'I don't know what I should have done if I'd lost them both—like that—so quickly.'

'I think it was my mother's death that caused my father's. They were very devoted to each other and he—well—he seemed to fade away after her death.' Thomas clamped the pipe between his teeth and lit it, inhaling deeply on it.

Caroline was thoughtful, trying to understand the bond of love that so tied two people together that the death of one could break the other's will to go on living. In her own society a marriage between two people was usually arranged by their respective parents who believed the match to be 'suitable' either by way of an amalgamation of properties, or a title married to wealth, or for some such mercenary reason. If the marriage partners were fortunate, an affection grew between them later. Occasionally—though rarely—they fell deeply in love with each other and were doubly blessed. That could not be said of her own mother and father, Caroline thought, though she did believe that they had been fond of each other and that a mutual respect and genuine friendship had existed between them. And certainly they had been united in their devotion to her, their only child. But now, as Caroline listened to Thomas Cole's deep voice speaking of the love between his parents, she realised that perhaps her own parents had missed experiencing the dizzy heights of a grand passion and a deep abiding love. Her romantic, girlish heart yearned to experience such a love.

The fact that Guy Trent danced with Sarah Miller four times during the course of the evening whilst only once with any other village girl escaped the notice of the ale-bemused villagers. All, that is, except one. Glowering resentfully, Henry Smithson observed his Sarah dancing so lightly, so expertly, with Guy Trent. There was nothing he could do about it. Guy Trent was the young master and Sarah was not betrothed to Henry. At least, not yet.

But she will be before this year is out, Henry vowed, and since there was scarcely a week of the old year left he would speak to her father the very next day.

Unaware of, or at least determinedly ignoring, Henry's sullen mood, Sarah danced on. Her eyes sparkled and in the flickering lights her white teeth glistened. Her cheeks were pink with the exertion of the dance and with excitement and pleasure. Watching Caroline dance with Guy Trent, Sarah had longed to change places with her, knowing that he too could dance just as well. And now here she was, Guy Trent, the handsome young master, looking at her as if she were the prettiest girl in the barn that night, and his sweet words of flirtation whispering into her willing ear. She was intoxicated by his flattery. It was the first time any man—except Henry and he didn't count being almost a cousin—had paid her such attention.

'Where've they been hiding you, Sarah Miller? You're the prettiest girl in the village. How is it I haven't seen you before a week or so ago when we met in the lane?'

Pertly she smiled and said, 'Oh I've been there, Master Guy, but you just haven't noticed me, that's all.'

Guy clasped his hands to his heart and threw back his head, giving a mock cry of agony. 'Oh, all that wasted time! You were there and I didn't see you! Sarah, my lovely Sarah!'

Gaily Sarah laughed, accepting his madcap compliments lightheartedly, and yet her heart quickened to see the look in his eyes, to feel the pressure of his fingers upon her hand. She tossed her flowing black hair and danced on, swaying, skipping, curtsying, flirting with the handsome young master. And all the time Henry Smithson watched them, the jealousy in his heart festering into hatred.

CHAPTER 4

Joseph Miller said, 'Aw Henry, she's too young yet to be promised to anyone. She's nobbut a lass. Besides, what have you to offer her, eh?'

Henry's scowl deepened. 'You've changed your tune all of a sudden. A bit back you'd have let 'er marry me to stop 'er goin' to the Grange.'

'Mebbe so. But you're Trent's man now, aren't you?' Joseph said scathingly.

'Ah—so *that's* it!'

Henry Smithson had been offered—and had accepted much to Joseph's disgust—the job Miller himself had refused, that of head cowman.

'But you're wrong, Joseph Miller, trying to fight the Trents. It's progress. Sir Matthew's building up his herd. One day he'll be famous for his cattle.'

'Ach!' Joseph flung out his arm in a gesture of dismissal. 'An' it'll be *your* labour that makes him famous—and puts money in his pocket!'

'An' if I'm well paid for it, why not?'
Joseph growled and turned away.

'An' if that is why you wun't let Sarah marry me,' Henry shouted after him. 'Because I work for the Trents, well, you want to watch out. Young Master Guy has his eye on her.'

Joseph spun round and walked back towards Henry, his fists clenched by his sides, menace in every step. Henry faced him fearlessly. He was younger, stronger, fitter than Joseph Miller.

'Just what d'you mean by that?'

'What I says. Didna you see him last night—at the barn? Four times he danced with Sarah. *Four times!*'

'I'll not have you speak her name in the same breath as his,' Joseph spat.

Henry shrugged. 'Well—I'm warning you. That's all.'

'Our Sarah's a good lass. She'd not be led on by 'im.'

Henry guffawed. 'She's had 'er head turned already by them up at the Grange.'

'Mind your tongue, Henry Smithson, when you speak of my Sarah.'

'Aw, Joseph, I've no wish to quarrel wi' you. You know how I feel for Sarah.'

Joseph's expression softened a little but

he was still on the defensive.

'I don't want no harm to come to 'er, that's all,' Henry added.

'It won't. I'll see to that.'

Henry sighed. Joseph Miller was a stubborn man, he thought, far-seeing in some things, but where his beloved Sarah was concerned he was completely blind!

Caroline could not forget the shy Thomas Cole. She was intrigued by him. Starved of any company of her own age and class in Abbeyford, his obvious, yet unspoken, admiration for her was an oasis in the desert of loneliness.

Her early-morning rides, which had for some time been routine, now took her down the hill to the bridge near the smithy, for the cottage beyond the smith and the wheelwright was where Thomas Cole lived. She found that he left home at eight o'clock each morning to begin his day's work. Late by some standards, but as estate bailiff and parish constable he varied his times of work according to the needs of the estate and village.

That first morning he saw her on the bridge seated side-saddle on her horse which pawed the ground restlessly, Thomas could not believe the good fortune that had brought him out of his cottage in time to see her pass. She was wearing an emerald green velvet riding habit, the jacket close-fitting whilst the full skirt fell in soft folds.

With a shock, Thomas realised she was not passing by, she was waiting on the bridge. He hesitated, uncertain what to do.

It could not be for him she waited, surely?

Caroline waved her riding-whip and Thomas Cole was drawn, unresisting, towards her. He raised his hat and bowed.

'Good-morning, Lady Caroline.'

'Good-morning, Mr Cole,' and then she added in a low whisper, *'Thomas!'*

He felt a jolt somewhere in the region of his heart as she murmured his name with such urgency. Then he heard her merry laugh.

'How formal we are this morning, Mr Cole! 'Twas not so that night at the barn.' She leant down from her horse and touched him lightly on the shoulder. 'Don't say you have forgotten that night already?'

'Oh no—no, my lady. I shall never, *never* forget that night,' he said softly.

Conscious that they were in full view of half the village, Thomas raised his hat again. 'I'll bid you a pleasant ride, m'lady,' and he made as if to move away.

'Thomas—I—I thought you rode about the estate?'

'That's right, m'lady.'

Smiling coquettishly she said, 'Then may I ride with you?'

He managed to answer, 'Yes—of course,' but his mind was in turmoil.

Every moment he spent in her company, he knew himself to be falling more and more in love with her. But where could that possibly lead? It could only end in unhappiness.

Still, he contented himself as he quickly saddled his own horse and joined her once more, a few hours in her company was better than only seeing her from afar.

Unassuming, modest Thomas Cole did not for one moment think that Lady Caroline could fall in love with him!

Every morning for the first two weeks of the New Year, Caroline rode away from the Grange, down the hill to the bridge to meet Thomas Cole. Together they rode around the estate for an hour or so and with each day that passed Thomas's love for Caroline deepened. But still he could not believe she cared for him.

'She's lonely,' he told himself. 'She just wants a companion on her rides.'

But he was wrong. Caroline decided that she loved Thomas Cole.

Soon one meeting a day was not enough. She began to take another ride in the afternoon around the hillsides and fields of Abbeyford searching for Thomas as he went about his duties as Sir Matthew Trent's estate bailiff.

And then—the snow came!

If Lady Caroline did all the running in the love-affair between herself and Thomas Cole, then the opposite was true in the case of Guy Trent and Sarah Miller. After the night of the celebrations in the barn at the Manor, she did not see him for over two weeks. Not that there were many times when he had chance to see her for she had very little freedom and, when she did visit her family in the village, suddenly Henry, or her father, seemed to be keeping a close watch upon her.

'You keep away from Master Guy,' her father had warned, worried by the doubts Henry's words had put into his mind. 'He's no good. He's got two young lasses from the village into trouble already.'

Sarah gasped. 'Pa! How can you say such a thing? You don't know.'

'Don't I, me girl? Why's Nell Potter and Meggie Owen disappeared all of a sudden then?'

'Well,' Sarah floundered, trying to find some explanation, some excuse. 'Mebbe they've gone into service—away from the village. Not all of 'em are as lucky as me to find work close by,' she reminded him artfully.

'Huh!' her father scoffed. 'Aye, that's the tale their families tell. But I knows different, see. You just do as I say, me girl, an' keep away from him. You attend to your work an' if you wants a young man you need look no further than young Henry.'

Sarah tossed her head. 'Anyway, I don't know why you think Guy Trent would ever look at the likes of me.' But even as she spoke the words she could not prevent the hope stealing into her mind that he would indeed look at the likes of her. She remembered, indeed clung to the memory of, the look in his eyes when he had danced with her.

Only two weeks into the New Year the snow came, falling steadily through a day and a night. Joseph Miller and Henry were out with the other men of the village rescuing the in-lamb ewes from the snowdrifts and bringing all the animals down to the buildings at the rear of the Manor.

Even Joseph Miller put aside his resentment against Sir Matthew when it came to rescuing animals.

On her half-day off, in the dusk of the winter afternoon, Guy Trent waited for Sarah beneath the snow-laden trees bordering the lane leading to the Grange.

Sarah trudged through the deep snow on her return to the Grange, her clog-encased little feet leaving deep gullies in the snow, her skirts soon sodden and clinging to her legs. She bent her head against the cold and concentrated on keeping to her feet.

She gave a cry of fright as she came up against something solid and looked up to find herself gazing into the laughing face of Guy Trent.

'Did I startle you, lovely Sarah?'

She gasped from the fright and from the cold, her breath like a puff of steam from her lips. 'Yes—yes you did.'

He took her hand in his and tucked her arm through his own. 'Come, there's a sheltered spot under the trees where we can—talk.'

Sarah made a half-hearted attempt to pull away. 'No—I must be getting back. I'll be in trouble if I'm late.'

'Just five minutes, Sarah,' he pleaded. 'Besides, you can't be expected to hurry through all this snow, now can you?' he added, reasonably enough.

Sarah allowed him to lead her to a shady spot under the trees, half of her wanting to stop and talk to him, the other half afraid of the consequences if her pa should find out.

'I've thought about you all the time since that night in the barn at Christmas.'

She gave a nervous laugh. 'That you haven't, Master Guy!'

'Indeed I have, lovely Sarah. I've been trying to see you. I've watched for you every week, but always your father or Henry Smithson has been with you.' He frowned. 'What is young Smithson to you,

Sarah? Are you betrothed to him?'

'No—no,' she shook her head quickly. 'He's my cousin—sort of.'

'Good.' Guy was smiling again. 'Then you're not promised to anyone?'

'Me?' she laughed and blushed. 'Of course not.'

'Why "of course not"? I'm surprised half the village lads aren't pounding on your door, lovely Sarah.'

Her blush deepened every time he called her 'lovely Sarah'. Was he mocking her, or did he, could he, really mean it?

'I mun go.' Now she did pull her hand away, but he caught her again.

'Meet me again, Sarah, please!' he begged urgently.

'I canna—I mustn't. I don't know how I could,' she added, weakening.

'Of course you can. Before you go home, come to the abbey ruins. The snow may have gone by next week. Look, I'll be waiting for you in the ruins midday every Wednesday.'

'No, no, I canna.' She pulled herself free of his grasp and floundered away from him through the snow.

'I'll be waiting, lovely Sarah,' he called after her.

I can't go, I mustn't go, she told herself fiercely, but with the sound of his voice ringing in her ears calling her 'lovely Sarah' she knew she would go!

CHAPTER 5

'Oh—this wretched snow! Will it never go?' moaned Caroline, restlessly pacing up and down in front of the long windows of the morning-room. 'Just look at it!'

For a whole week she had been unable to go riding—unable to meet Thomas. She had grown irritable, feeling a prisoner, trapped by the bad weather.

Then she stopped and peered out of the window. 'Goodness—whatever is this coming? Why, it's Lynwood!' She clapped her hands in delight. 'Oh do look, Papa, he's driving a sledge pulled by two ponies. Oh, how clever of him!'

She whirled around, picked up her skirts and ran from the room. 'Tell him to wait for me...'

The young Lord Lynwood was shown into the morning-room. Lord Royston greeted him warmly. 'Why, Lynwood, how good to see you!' His eyes twinkled merrily. 'My daughter instructs me to ask you to wait for her. I think she rather fancies a ride in your—er—new mode of transport.'

Lynwood laughed. 'That's why I came—I was rather hoping she might.'

Lady Caroline appeared dressed in a dark blue velvet coat and holding a warm fur muff. Perched upon her head was a hat with three fluttering plumes.

'Good-morning, Caroline.' Lynwood's blue eyes were full of devotion. 'I came to see if you would care to come skating. Our lake is completely frozen over.'

'Oh Francis—I'd love it!' she cried, but Lord Royston frowned.

'Are you sure it's safe, Lynwood? The ice is not always as thick as it seems.'

'Yes, my lord. I've already tried it out.'

'Very well then. But take care.'

Minutes later they were in the sledge.

'Francis—this is wonderful,' Caroline laughed as the sharp air stung her face bringing a rosy glow to her cheeks. 'How clever you are to think of such a scheme! I have not been out of the Grange for over a week and I've been so *bored!*'

They flew across the snow, the sure-footed ponies never faltering. As they passed by the village, Caroline scanned the snow-covered fields, but to her disappointment there was no sign of Thomas.

As Lynwood had said, the lake in front of Lynwood Hall was frozen over.

'I'll have to hold on to you, Francis,' Caroline said, as Lynwood bent to tie on her skates for her. 'I remember skating here once—but I was only eight or nine. Your poor papa took me on to the ice.'

Lynwood stood up, his face sober.

Caroline squeezed his arm. 'I know how you must miss him, for I miss my dear mama. But come, let's not think such morbid thoughts today. You must teach me to skate. Show me first what I should do.'

Lynwood stepped on to the ice and skated steadily around in a circle, then he returned to Caroline and held out his hands. 'Take hold of my hands.'

Caroline giggled and stepped on to the ice. It was a peculiar sensation, feeling not quite in control of her feet. She clung on to Lynwood whilst he pulled her round the ice.

'Now you try sliding each foot forward—that's it.'

'Oh Francis—this is fun!'

Young Lynwood slipped his arm about her waist to guide her, for, although he was four years her junior, already he was half a head taller than Caroline.

'Oh, oh I'm falling,' she cried and clutched at him.

'I've got you—you're all right.'

It was one of the happiest afternoons Lynwood could remember. He had Caroline all to himself. She laughed and talked with him as her equal, clinging to his arm for support.

As the bright winter day faded into gloom, Lynwood took her into the Hall for a glass of hot punch before taking her back to the Grange in his sledge.

'Thank you, Francis. It was sweet of you to take me skating.'

Lynwood smiled and gallantly raised her fingers to his lips.

As he watched her go into the Grange, he thought that in four or five years' time when he came to manhood the difference in their ages would not seem so great.

Lynwood returned home with a secret hope locked within his heart.

The snow was slow to clear and Sarah passed the week following her meeting with Guy in the lane in a ferment of indecision. She wanted the snow to melt away so that she could go to the abbey ruins to meet him and yet she half-wished that more snow would fall so heavily that she could not possibly get there!

But by the following Wednesday most of the snow had gone. Frozen patches still blotched the fields but the way to the abbey ruins was clear.

A little after midday Sarah left Abbeyford Grange but instead of taking her usual way home down the lane she ran down the slope in front of the big house and crossed the stream by a footbridge. Skirting the village she walked through the meadow and joined the lane leading out of the village up towards the Manor. She came to the ford in the road and to the narrow footbridge, the only means by which a traveller on foot might cross the water. The stream was swollen with melting snow and the wooden boards of the bridge were only just visible above the water and every few moments the water lapped right over them. Sarah swallowed and glanced about her fearfully.

There was no one about, no one who had seen her come this far. She looked up towards the abbey ruins standing black and gaunt and lonely against the lowering sky. Was he there? Was Guy waiting for her? Or was she making a complete fool of herself.

She bit her lip and stepped gingerly on to the bridge. Holding tightly on to the handrail she picked her way carefully across, but the water splashed against her boots and caught the hem of her skirt. Again she looked about her and, seeing no one, she bent her head and hurried up the lane towards the Manor, but instead of turning into the stable-yard she scurried past, on up the hill and into the wood. Here beneath the shadow of the trees Sarah breathed more easily. But there was still the open space between the wood and the abbey ruins to cross. At the edge of the wood she paused. If she ran across the space to the ruins she was clearly visible from the valley though, at this distance, scarcely recognisable. If she walked a little further to the right, she thought, she would not be so easily seen for, although the land did not actually slope away on this side but continued in an undulating plateau until it dropped again into the village of Amberly, at least she would be out of sight of the village. And on this side were the Lynwood lands, so anyone in these fields seeing her would not be interested.

Picking up her skirts and drawing a deep breath she ran from the edge of the wood in a wide arc and eventually came into the abbey ruins from the opposite side to that overlooking Abbeyford. Breathless she leant against the crumbling walls, drawing the cold air into her lungs in huge gasps. As long as her pa or Henry hadn't seen her!

She peered into the ruins and shivered. The wind howled around the broken-down walls, moaning like the ghosts of long ago, and Sarah, fanciful and superstitious, would have turned and run away if she had not seen Guy Trent's chestnut horse tethered by the far wall.

Her heart gave a leap. He was here. He was waiting for her. Then she saw him, standing on one of the low walls, looking out over Abbeyford, watching for her.

She drew her cloak around her and stepped into the ruins, over the ground littered with stones and boulders. He heard her crunching step and turned round.

Seeing her, he grinned, leapt down from the wall and ran towards her.

'You came!' he said placing his hands upon her shoulders and smiling down into her dark, fearful eyes.

'Yes,' she whispered. 'But I shouldn't have.'

'Oh Sarah, who's to know?'

'I canna get away so easily. Me ma will be expecting me.'

'Say you were delayed.'

'But what if anyone saw me coming up here?'

'They didn't—did they?'

'Not that I know of, but...'

'Lovely Sarah, don't frown so.' He smoothed her forehead with his fingers, as if to brush away her worries. 'Come—over here. It's warmer.'

He drew her into a small, cell-like room, the only one left whole in the ruins, with only a narrow window, high up, and the doorway to let in any light.

Sarah swallowed her apprehension as she saw that there were dried rushes upon the floor. Guy must have prepared this place for her—for them.

'Here—sit down, Sarah.' He spread his own cloak over the rushes and as she sat down he dropped down beside her. He put his arm about her shoulders and pulled her to him. 'There, that's warmer, isn't it?'

She nodded. She was where she wanted to be—with Guy. Yet she could not still the fear, the knowledge, that she was doing wrong. She was afraid of what he might do. But Guy just sat with his arm about her shoulders, holding her close for warmth, making no attempt to kiss her, just talking to her, so that gradually she began to relax against him.

'Do you like it up at the Grange? Are they good to you?'

'Oh yes,' Sarah told him eagerly. 'Lady Caroline's lovely. He's nice, his lordship, but a bit severe, an' I don't see much of him anyway.'

Guy sighed. 'What a pity it's not my mother you work for, then I could see a good deal more of you.' He gave her shoulders a squeeze and again Sarah felt that peculiar thrill run through her—half fear, half delight.

'I should be going,' she murmured, but she made no effort to move.

'Not yet.' Guy's face was close to hers in the half-light of the tiny room.

Time passed more quickly than she

realised in his company and, when next she thought about leaving, she looked towards the slit of a window and saw to her horror that it was already growing dusk.

She scrambled to her feet. 'Oh it's late. I'll be missed. I'll be in trouble.'

Guy too got up. 'Sarah, Sarah, don't run away.'

'I must, I must!' Wildly she pulled away from his reaching hands and squeezed out of the doorway and began to stumble across the rubble-strewn ground.

'Sarah! Sarah!' He caught up with her and grasped at her arm. 'When will you come again?'

'I don't know, I don't know!' she cried, unable to think clearly, the only thought in her head being to get home before it grew dark, before her pa and Henry came home. Henry would come to their house tonight straight from his work, knowing it was her half-day off.

As she hurried out of the ruins and began to run across the intervening space towards the wood, completely forgetting this time to hide herself from the valley, she heard him call.

'Next week, Sarah. Please!'

Sarah hurried on, her head bent against

the blustering wind which now blew flecks of snow against her, stinging her cheeks and catching her breath.

Through the wood and down the lane past the Manor. She hurried towards the footbridge and then stopped in dismay. The water now completely covered the planking of the footbridge. In that short time the water had risen that last vital inch or so and now covered the wooden boards of the bridge. Panic rose in her throat and her knees began to tremble. She was trapped on the wrong side of the stream and it was already growing dark. This was the only way across the stream into the village.

It couldn't be so very deep, she tried to reason. She glanced back up the lane. If only someone would come along with a cart, she could beg a lift through the ford. But now, when she wanted someone to appear, the lane was still empty.

Sarah bit her lip and glanced at the threatening sky; the flecks of snow had turned to rain now and it was coming faster. Soon there would be even more volume added to the already swollen stream. Sarah took a resolute breath and picked up her skirts almost to her knees and stepped into the water. She gasped as it swirled above her ankle-boots and clutched icy fingers at her legs. She reached for the handrail and breathed a sigh of relief as she felt its roughness beneath her fingers. Slowly she inched her way along, feeling with each foot for the hidden boards beneath. She was about halfway across and thinking she was going to make it when her foot slipped and almost before she realised she had fallen she was floundering in the freezing stream, gasping for breath. The stream bowled her over and over, bruising her arms and legs, and a stone cut her chin. She spluttered and gulped and then, feeling the bottom, she managed to stand upright. It wasn't as deep as she had feared, only to her thighs, but the shock of falling into the cold water and the unusual swiftness of the flow of the stream had made her think she was in more danger than she actually was.

Sobbing, she dragged herself out of the water, her clothes clinging to her in a sodden mass. She squelched the rest of the way home and fell thankfully through the door into the warmth of the cottage kitchen.

Her mother, lifting bread from the brick oven, threw up her hands in horror.

'Oh my dear child! Whatever's happened? I thought you weren't coming today, it bein' so late now. Where have you been?' She hurried towards the shivering Sarah and drew her towards the fire. 'Here, strip these clothes off an' I'll get you a blanket. You'll catch your death, else.'

'No, Ma, I canna. Pa an' Henry...'

'Never mind them. They can stay out till you're finished. I'll not have you catch cold, me girl.'

Soon Sarah was sitting with a rough blanket wrapped around her, whilst her mother rubbed her wet hair. Guiltily Sarah accepted her mother's ministrations.

'What happened?' her mother asked again, towelling her dry with skin-reddening briskness.

'I—I fell in the stream. The water's over the bridge.'

Her mother stopped her rubbing and stared at her in amazement. 'What, Smithy's Bridge?' Mrs Miller referred to the stone bridge near the smithy.

'No—no.'

'I didna think it could be. Why, if that were under water then the whole village'd be flooded!' She thought for a moment then added, 'You weren't daft enough to come by the field bridge—the one behind the village?'

'Well—yes, I did. But it weren't that one.'

'Well then?'

'The—the footbridge—near the ford.'

'Lord, girl! What were you doin' near that un? It dunna take much to put that un under water—you *know* that!' she added scathingly to a girl born and bred in Abbeyford. Miserably Sarah nodded.

'What were you doin' that way, anyway?'

Sarah took a deep breath. 'I—er—had to take a message to—to the Manor.'

'Huh!' Mrs Miller resumed her vigorous rubbing. ' 'Tain't right. Askin' a young girl to go traipsin' round the countryside in weather like this. I've a mind to...'

'No, Ma, please!' Sarah cried, frightened that her lie would lead her into deeper trouble. 'Dunna say nothing—please.'

'Well,' said her mother doubtfully, 'I don't want to do anything to make you lose that good job you've got, but still...'

'Please, Ma,' Sarah begged.

'Very well, then, but I dunna know what your pa will say.' Sarah was silent. She too was worried what her pa would say!

Joseph Miller had plenty to say—but not what his wife had expected.

'She's lying!' he exploded, thumping the table with his fist, whilst Sarah jumped physically and her mother gasped in astonishment. 'Joseph...!'

'I tell you, she's lying. They wouldn't send a young maid on such an errand. They've footmen and stable-boys for that. Just where did you go, girl?' he demanded, leaning towards her menacingly.

'I—I told you,' Sarah stammered.

Beth said slyly, 'I reckon I saw Master Guy Trent riding across the brow of the hill towards the abbey ruins this afternoon.'

That was all she needed to say for the colour that swept into Sarah's face gave her away.

'You little bitch!' Joseph Miller spat and raised his hand to strike her across the face, but his wife stepped between them.

'Joseph, I will not have such language in this house. And don't strike the girl till you know the truth.' She rounded on Beth. 'And you, miss, I know your vicious tongue. As for you...' She whipped round to Sarah now and grasped her by her long black hair. 'We'll have the truth now. Well?'

When Sarah did not answer at once, her mother pulled her hair hard. 'Answer me, girl.'

'Yes—yes—*yes!*' The admission was torn from her and then she sank to the floor in a sobbing heap.

Her mother stood over her, her lips pursed, whilst Joseph growled, 'There, I knew it!' and Beth merely smiled, maliciously satisfied. In her corner, Ella, the youngest sister, crooned softly to her doll oblivious of the drama taking place in front of her uncomprehending eyes.

'You're a little fool, Sarah. You'll not meet him again. You promise me now? He's no good, d'you hear me?'

Still sobbing, Sarah nodded.

Mrs Miller turned towards her husband, taking charge of the situation now. 'You or Henry will meet her each week from the Grange and see her back.' She glanced down at her eldest daughter, then looked at her husband. 'Say no more about it now. I reckon she's learnt her lesson.'

She stepped over Sarah and began laying

the table for supper, but Joseph's face still scowled.

He was not so sure his wayward daughter would obey.

CHAPTER 6

When the snow cleared, Lady Caroline resumed her own secret meetings—with Thomas Cole. Soon all the village were aware of the growing attachment between them. Only Lord Royston remained in ignorance. The villagers shook their heads over the matter, foreseeing only tragedy at such an unsuitable liaison.

'Someone should tell his lordship!' was the general opinion. But who? Who would dare to tell the Earl of Royston that his beloved only daughter was keeping company with his tenant farmer's bailiff?

Caroline played a meticulous game of hide and seek. Seeking out Thomas whilst at the same time hiding from her father, who himself frequently rode about the estate offering advice to Sir Matthew, or giving orders to his own gamekeeper.

Always she had an excuse ready in case she should be questioned. She made frequent visits to Lynwood Hall in the hope of being able to meet Thomas on the way back. But this ploy was often thwarted for Lynwood would escort her home and spoil her plans.

At one time she had enjoyed basking in Lynwood's obvious adoration of her. Now she found his devotion irksome. His insistence on accompanying her prevented her from seeing Thomas!

'There's really no need for you to come all the way back to the Grange with me, Francis. I am quite able to take care of myself.'

'We still get vagabonds and paupers along the roads—even in Abbeyford and Amberly,' Lynwood told her seriously.

Caroline laughed rather cruelly. 'And if we were set upon—just what do you think *you* could do? You're only a boy!'

She slapped her riding-crop against her horse's flanks and galloped ahead of him, into the woods above Abbeyford.

She could not have hurt young Lynwood more if she had plunged a knife into his heart!

He reined in and sat watching her

gallop away from him, her wide skirt billowing, her long auburn hair flying free.

As she disappeared amongst the trees, he turned his horse around and returned home, the secret hope in his heart shattered.

Caroline found a further excuse for riding down into Abbeyford with the arrival in the village of her cousin, Martha.

Martha was indeed 'the poor relation'. She was the daughter of Caroline's mother's sister and so the connection with the Earl of Royston was rather distant. But that did not prevent Martha feeling resentful that her cousin Caroline should be a lady of quality whilst she herself was a mere curate's wife. Lord Royston had been prevailed upon by his late wife's sister to offer the living at Abbeyford to her son-in-law, the Reverend Hugh Langley.

So the recently married Langleys had moved into Abbeyford Vicarage.

'It's a lovely house, Martha.' Caroline viewed the rooms critically.

Martha sniffed, folding her hands in front of her. 'It will no doubt be cold and draughty. These huge vicarages always are.'

'Oh come now, my dear,' Hugh remonstrated gently. 'Pray don't let your cousin think us ungrateful.' He turned his pale eyes on Caroline. 'I am indebted to your father. I never thought to gain such a living so soon.'

'It's no more than you deserve, Hugh,' Martha snapped. 'Why must you always belittle yourself so?'

Hugh Langley was a mild, gentle, rather fussy little man. At thirty he already stooped slightly from the long hours he had spent poring over his books, studying hard. His mousy-coloured hair was thinning and his face was pale from lack of sunshine and fresh air.

Hesitantly he said. 'There was just one more thing—er—I was wondering if there are any boys locally who might benefit from—well—private tuition?'

Caroline wrinkled her brow thoughtfully. 'Guy Trent's a little old now.' She laughed. 'And he's scarcely the studious type anyway. There is Francis, Lord Lynwood. He's about fourteen.'

'No doubt they'll already have some arrangement for his education,' put in the pessimistic Martha.

'His father's dead, but I'll ask Lady Lynwood the next time I see her.'

'Thank you—thank you,' Hugh said fussily, almost bowing towards Lady Caroline, but Martha merely pursed her already thin lips.

'As a matter of fact, that's an excellent idea, Caroline,' Lady Lynwood beamed. 'I have been looking for a tutor for Francis. I must confess, Caroline, that although I should send him away to school I fear I am far too selfish to rob myself of his company. Your cousin's husband sounds admirably suitable.'

Caroline laughed. 'Oh, Mr Langley is the typical 'professor' type. Very muddly over everyday living and completely dominated by my cousin, Martha.' Caroline wrinkled her nose a little. 'She's a bit of a shrew, but I believe he's really quite clever academically.'

'Good—good. Ah Francis, there you are,' Lady Lynwood greeted her young son as he sidled into the room, his blue eyes intent upon Caroline.

Caroline smiled at him. 'Good-day, Francis.'

'Lady Caroline,' he muttered and listened politely whilst his mother said, 'Caroline has found you a tutor. The new vicar at Abbeyford is her cousin's husband.'

Francis nodded, but his gaze did not divert from Caroline's face. Though he still looked upon her with adoration, now there was a haunted, hurt expression deep within his eyes. The fact that it was Caroline who had found a tutor for him was yet a further reminder of the difference in their ages. He was still regarded as a schoolboy, whilst she was out of the classroom, an adult young lady.

Lady Lynwood, sensitive to her son's feelings for Caroline, was immediately aware of the subtle change in him. She could see in an instant that in some way Caroline had hurt her son.

Caroline stood up. 'I must be going. There's a meet of the hunt next week, I believe, now the snow has gone. Will you be following in your carriage as usual, Lady Lynwood?'

The older woman nodded. 'Most definitely. Francis is to be bloodied. I mustn't miss that.'

'Neither must I.' Caroline turned to the boy. 'I'll be sure to watch out for you,' she told him and the colour rose faintly in his cheeks and the pain in his eyes lessened a little.

Lady Lynwood sighed within herself. There was nothing she could do to help him, but she wished that her son were not so easily affected by Caroline's volatile moods. One kind word from her could make him happy, one cruel word could make him miserable.

Lynwood accompanied Caroline to the front door and down the steps. He watched her mount her horse and canter away down the drive.

Behind him he heard two of the stable-lads sniggering together. Then clearly their conversation drifted to his ears.

'My Lady Caroline off to meet her lover. Master Thomas Cole aims high!'

Lynwood turned, rage flooding through him. He couldn't understand the full meaning of their words because he knew nothing of her affair with the bailiff. But he recognised by the inflection in their voices that they were insulting Caroline.

Without hesitation, Lynwood launched himself towards the two boys, fists flying. Caught unawares, one fell beneath his blows, his nose bloodied. The other received a blow beneath the ribs which doubled him up and he sank to his knees.

'You are dismissed from my employ and will be off the Lynwood estate by nightfall!'

Breathing hard, Lynwood turned and marched back into the house. The two boys, nursing their injuries, stared after him in amazement.

'What did us do? What did us *say?*' they asked each other.

Caroline rode away from Lynwood Hall, back through Amberly towards Abbeyford. But once in the wooded shade at the top of the hill she left the track leading through the wood to Abbeyford, turning in the opposite direction from the abbey ruins. She followed a rough footpath as far as possible and then slid from her horse's back and tethered him to a tree. Delicately lifting her skirt she ran lightly down a steep narrow path, twisting and turning through the trees until she came to a waterfall bubbling down a steep rock face into a deep pool and then tumbling on down the hillside until it became the stream which meandered through Abbeyford valley.

Caroline sat down upon a rock, watching the waterfall. With all the recent snow added to its normal flow, it was fast-flowing and the pool deeper than ever. Caroline shivered and drew her cloak around her and hoped Thomas would soon join her.

They met in different places around Abbeyford. Sometimes here at the waterfall. Sometimes in the abbey ruins. Sometimes they each rode out of Abbeyford, well away from the prying eyes of the villagers, meeting in the fields and lanes, in tiny copses or derelict shepherds' huts.

She heard a rustle on the pathway and jumped up to meet him as Thomas appeared through the trees. She ran towards him flinging her arms around him with passionate abandon.

'Thomas, oh Thomas. It seems an age since I saw you and yet it was only yesterday. Kiss me!' She clung to him, winding her arms around his neck.

Never ceasing to wonder why this adorable creature should imagine herself in love with him, Thomas held her close, kissing her tenderly and then finding himself responding ardently to her feverish desire.

'Thomas, oh my Thomas! If only we could be together for always,' she murmured.

Thomas smiled gently but a little sadly. He could not believe that her love for him would last. He told himself that loneliness had driven her to seek him out, that once the London season began again he would be swiftly forgotten. He loved her, he knew, but he could not believe that there would be a future for them together.

Caroline was determined that it should be otherwise.

'Thomas, listen!' She took his hand and led him to the rock. Together they sat down side by side. 'I've been thinking. We cannot go on like this.'

There, he knew it! And although he had always told himself it would end he could not stop the swift, painful stab in his heart.

'I think I should tell my father that—that we love each other.'

Fear washed over him. 'Caroline, my love—no!'

Caroline's eyes widened. 'Why ever not? Thomas—you do love me, don't you?'

'Oh my darling.' He reached out and

touched her cheek wonderingly, adoringly. 'You'll never know how much.'

'And you do want to marry me, don't you?'

The turmoil of emotions showed upon his face. Torn between the exquisite longing to make her his wife and the knowledge that it was impossible. His voice was a hoarse whisper. 'Caroline—it can never be.'

'Why ever not?' she demanded fiercely, her pretty mouth pouting as it did when she was about to be thwarted in something she wanted. She jumped angrily to her feet. 'You're making excuses. You don't want to marry me. You—you don't love me! You're—you're just playing with my affections!'

Thomas rose to his feet, holding out his arms pleadingly towards her. It was the first time he had seen her angry and it frightened his gentle, loving nature. 'Caroline—you know that is not true. You know I love you more than life itself, but your father...'

Caroline flung herself against him again. 'Oh Thomas, I'm sorry.' She covered his face with kisses. 'Forgive me. Don't let us quarrel, I can't bear it if we quarrel. I know you mean to protect me. But he will have to know sometime.'

Thomas sighed. He knew what would happen. Caroline would be confined to her home and he would be dismissed and sent away from Abbeyford. He voiced none of these fears to her. She could not see that her father would deny her anything, but Thomas knew that Lord Royston, despite his indulgence towards his daughter, would never countenance this liaison. His anger would fall upon his daughter as never before, though she could not realise it.

'I must go.' Reluctantly she withdrew from the shelter of his fond embrace. 'Till tomorrow, my love. We'll meet in the abbey ruins tomorrow—the same time.'

Once more she kissed him, pressing her young body to him, causing Thomas's head to reel and driving all sensible thoughts from his mind.

'Till tomorrow,' she whispered, turned away and ran up the path.

Thomas waited for some minutes before he too left the shelter of the glade and returned to Abbeyford by a roundabout route.

The hunt met in the stable-yard at Abbeyford Manor.

Lady Lynwood, with Caroline beside her, watched from her open carriage.

It was a fine sight—the scarlet coats and high top-hats of the huntsmen, the horses groomed to shining perfection. The hounds, which were kennelled at the Manor, were fine brown and white dogs, strong and eager for the chase to begin, their tails held high, their pink tongues lolling.

'There's Francis! Oh doesn't he look splendid?' Caroline waved eagerly to the young boy, who was seated, straight-backed, on his mount. 'You must be very proud of your son, Lady Lynwood. I'm sure he'll break a few hearts when he grows up.'

Lady Lynwood laughed—a delicious cackling sound, quite unladylike but infectious to anyone hearing it. She patted Caroline's hand. ' 'Tis a pity he's not older for I know he admires you greatly.'

Caroline laughed too. 'He'll be a fine man one day and she'll be a lucky girl who catches him, but I'm afraid I can't wait that long.'

Her eyes strayed to where Thomas Cole

sat astride his horse. How elegant he looked, how solemn and so aware of the privilege he had been given in being allowed to join the hunt which was, after all, made up mainly of wealthy landowners or their respected tenant farmers! For Thomas Cole to be one of their number was an unusual compliment to the man.

Lynwood, ever acutely aware of Caroline's nearness, saw her watching Thomas Cole. Young though he was, because of his own feelings for her Lynwood easily recognised the expression of love upon her face as she watched Thomas Cole.

Lynwood frowned. So, he thought bitterly, the stable-boys' gossip had not been without foundation.

The cry went up, 'They're moving off!' and then the horses and hounds moved out of the yard, watched by the half-dozen or more grooms and stable-lads who looked after Sir Matthew's horses and the hounds belonging to the hunt.

Down the lane they cantered and into the fields, the hounds streaming out ahead of the huntsmen, trying to pick up the scent of a fox.

Guy Trent, reckless as ever, galloped ahead, to the annoyance of his father, but young Lynwood, though this was his first meet, had been well-schooled in the etiquette of the hunting field and stayed well to the back. He rode well and easily, but his mind was not on the chase. Before him was the picture of Caroline's face when she looked at Thomas Cole!

Over hedges and ditches the horses flew, through the two streams and up the hill, the hounds spreading out. Suddenly there was a shrill barking and the dogs streaked forward. The hunting-horn sounded and they were off up the hill past Abbeyford Grange and over the brow.

Lady Lynwood flicked her reins and the carriage moved forward. 'We'll follow at a more sedate pace, my dear,' she said.

Sarah Miller saw the hunt pass the Grange. Leaning out of a second-floor window, she saw Guy Trent, his head down, his body pressed close to his horse, galloping like a mad thing after the baying hounds. She watched him, admiring his daring but at the same time fearing for his safety because she loved him. She saw them all pass by and reach the top of the hill above the

Grange and then they were gone out of sight, only the sounds of the dogs and the drumming hoofbeats were left, growing fainter and fainter.

She leaned her face against the cool casement of the window. Yes—she loved Guy Trent. But what a hopeless, foolish love it was!

Guy Trent, eager to secure the brush as his trophy, rode, knife in hand, amongst the hounds as they closed upon the fox, after a long and gruelling chase.

'Damn the boy!' Sir Matthew muttered. 'Has he no sense? He'll cripple my best hounds.'

Lynwood, though he would dearly have loved to secure the brush to present to Caroline, held back.

As Guy triumphantly held aloft the severed tail, his father beckoned him. Extricating himself from the excited, barking dogs was not without hazard and Guy felt more than one nip on his legs. But his prize of the day justified a little discomfort.

Sir Matthew held out his hand towards his son.

Guy's face darkened. 'The brush is mine, sir.'

'I think not. As Master I have the right to bestow it upon whosoever I choose in the field.'

Father and son glared at each other; Sir Matthew with his hand still extended waited.

With a growl of annoyance, Guy almost flung the brush at his father and turned away. He mounted his horse and galloped—hot-headed as ever—away from the field.

'Here, my boy,' Sir Matthew turned towards Lynwood. 'This is yours. You have carried yourself well today. Your father would have been proud of you—very proud.'

The boy smiled and accepted the brush.

Lady Lynwood and Caroline caught up with the hunt just after the kill, in time to see young Francis initiated. They watched as Sir Matthew passed the bloody head of the decapitated fox across the boy's forehead and down each cheek, the brilliant red blood stark against the paleness of the boy's skin. He stood erect, proud, almost haughty, making not a sound.

Lady Lynwood smiled with pride at her son as he remounted his horse and rode over to her carriage. How mature he looked today, far older than his fourteen years!

'Well done, my son, well done!' She reached over and squeezed his hand.

Caroline smiled at the boy. 'Indeed, Francis, you are a credit to us all.'

Shyly he held out the brush to Caroline. 'I—would like you to have this.'

'Why, Francis, how sweet of you to give me your very first trophy!'

She took the brush and smiled at him. She could see his adoration for her in his eyes. 'Why, Francis, you're quite the gallant.'

Lady Lynwood looked on but said nothing. Her son's feeling for Caroline was a fragile, vulnerable thing and young Lynwood could be so easily hurt — desperately hurt—if Caroline were to ridicule his devotion to her.

Fond though she was of the daughter of her dear friends, Lady Lynwood was sensible enough to see the selfish, even ruthless, streak in Caroline's nature and knew the girl would always want her own way and care little for the feelings of others who might try to thwart her desires!

CHAPTER 7

Winter gave way to Spring reluctantly, but at last the days grew warmer and Nature's life-cycle began again. As the trees blossomed so did the love between Guy Trent and Sarah Miller. Perhaps it was because it was a forbidden love that it made their stolen moments all the more precious, the excitement of furtive meetings, the danger of further discovery fuelling their passion for each other.

For several weeks after Joseph Miller had found out that Sarah was meeting Guy, she had no opportunity of seeing him, for every week on her days off either Joseph or Henry would meet her from the Grange, escort her home and accompany her up the lane again in the evening.

She knew Guy was trying to reach her. Twice, as she returned to Abbeyford Grange, her father striding along at the side of her, she heard the soft whinnying of a horse hidden amongst the trees which bordered the lane. She felt her father's eyes upon her, but he said nothing and she, head down, walked on in silence, but her heart was leaping wildly within her, her legs trembling at the thought of Guy's closeness.

As the days lengthened, work on the estate increased—and the fences began to go up on the common waste-land. Joseph Miller watched with resentful eyes.

'I mun sell my cows an' sheep, Ellen,' he told his wife, hardly able to keep the savagery he felt inside from showing in his tone.

'Oh no, Joseph!' Her eyes were wide with fear.

He shrugged. 'We've still got your spinning and perhaps...'

'Joseph—there's—there's something I've been meaning to tell you, but—but—I hadn't got around to it.' Her fingers plucked nervously at her apron.

He had never seen his wife act this way before, as if she were afraid of him. Gently he took her by the shoulders. 'Why, Ellen, what is it, wife? Aw, I know I've been difficult of late—it's the Trents...' With an effort he swallowed his own anger and spoke tenderly to his wife. Tears welled up in her eyes. His Ellen, who never wept whatever harsh blows life inflicted upon her!

Joseph was shocked.

He gave her a gentle little shake. 'Come, tell me what ails you?'

'It's the spinning work, Joseph. There's a new man been round. A Mister Lewis. He—he says they're installing some new-fangled machinery in the factory an' cutting down on the cottagers in this district doin' the work. He said it's—un—uneconomical—yes, that was the word he used.'

Joseph's fingers tightened on her shoulders and his eyes flashed with renewed indignation. 'An' it's a sight more "uneconomical" for us! Him an' his fancy words! Dun't he know he's robbin' us of our livelihood? Just how much are they cutting down?'

'Well...' Ellen hesitated and avoided meeting his gaze, then she whispered. 'Next month'll be the last he brings any.'

'You mean he's stopping all of it?'

Ellen nodded. 'Joseph—I'm sorry.'

'Aw Ellen, it's not your fault. But—what are we to do?'

Ellen, always the family's will of iron, its rock, was for once lost.

Joseph loosed his grip on her shoulders,

turned away and sat down heavily in the chair at the side of the hearth. 'I'll have to look for work away from Abbeyford. I canna get work here. Not now. Trent as good as told me.' Bitterly, his mouth tight, he added, 'I shouldn't be surprised if Trent hasn't had a hand in this other business an' all.'

'Oh Joseph, surely not. Why, Mr Lewis is naught to do with the Trents.'

Joseph shrugged. 'Aye, but them 'n all their kind are in league agen us and Trent as good as threatened me with it!'

'Joseph—what are we to do?' Ellen whispered.

'As long as he dunna turn us out of our home, I can find work.'

'There's Sarah's money. She's very good, Joseph, she only keeps a penny or two for hersel'.'

Joseph's face was grim. He still did not like to be reminded of Sarah's employment at the Grange, but for the moment it was all they had to live on.

The next morning—very early—found Joseph trudging up the hill out of the valley in the hope of finding work away from Abbeyford. He would not be able to meet Sarah on her half-days off, he thought, as every step took him further and further away from his family. Henry too would be too busy now that Sir Matthew was increasing the size of his herd, but Joseph comforted himself with the belief that with the lapse of time since she had last seen Guy Trent he would have forgotten all about little Sarah Miller and found himself fresh amusement.

Joseph was wrong. The very fact that Sarah was being kept from him only served to make Guy want her more. If he had but understood the nature of Guy Trent, Joseph's action was the very one to inflame the young man's interest. Had he left things as they were, perhaps Guy's ardour would have quickly waned. As it was, her elusiveness was a challenge—a challenge the madcap Guy could not resist.

Sarah skipped down the lane from Abbeyford Grange on her own for the first time in weeks.

She gave a little cry of fright as she heard a rustle amongst the trees and saw the stealthy figure of a man. Then, as he emerged into the lane, happiness flooded through her. It was Guy! He held out his arms to her and without a moment's hesitation she ran into his embrace.

'Sarah, oh Sarah. They shouldn't have kept you from me. They shouldn't have!' he murmured with a rare insight into his own character.

'Oh Guy, I missed you so,' Sarah whispered, completely without guile or affectation. He was raining kisses on her face, on her smooth brow, her eyelids, her soft, rosy cheeks and her delicious mouth. She clung to him, yielding herself to him.

'Where can we go?' he murmured against her mouth. 'How can we meet? I can't go on living without you.'

Breathless, Sarah said, 'They'll come with me whenever they can. I don't know why one of them isn't here today.' Almost fearful that either Joseph or Henry might suddenly appear, she glanced over her shoulder.

'Can you slip out—at night—from the Grange?' Guy asked urgently. 'I could be waiting—anytime—anywhere.'

'I don't—know. I could try,' she said eagerly. 'The servants all go to bed about ten o'clock. Sometimes Lady Caroline wants me later, but—not often.'

'Can you get out without being seen?' Tenderly he stroked her black hair away from her forehead, looking down into her upturned face.

'I'll try, oh I'll try,' she breathed.

'Tonight. Behind the stables at the side of the Grange. I'll be waiting,' he told her. Reluctantly he let her go, watching her hurry away down the lane towards the village.

'See what your precious Guy Trent and his father have done to us now?' Beth was the first to meet Sarah with the news of the recent disaster which had overtaken the Miller family. 'We'll be out on the street next!'

Sarah did not answer. Nothing—but nothing—could dim the glow in her heart at the thought of meeting Guy that very night.

That night and many nights following, Sarah crept from her warm bed, out into the dark night and into the arms of her lover.

Towards the end of April the maypole was set up on the village green and on the evening of the last day of April an excited, laughing party of village youths and girls set off for the wood at the top of the hill to gather green branches and spring flowers to weave into garlands to decorate their homes and the maypole. Mayday was a day of celebration in the village. It marked the beginning of summer for the country folk, of warmer days, of new life and growth.

Among the revellers were Sarah Miller and Henry Smithson. Henry was in a particularly jovial mood. Tonight and for the whole of the next day he and Sarah could be together and by the end of that time, he vowed, he would have made her promise to marry him.

The woods soon echoed with laughter, with squeals and furtive giggles as the young men stole kisses from their sweethearts. Many a new courtship began at Mayday and resulted in marriage before the year was out.

Henry slipped his arm around Sarah's waist and felt her stiffen.

'Oh, come on, our Sarah. No one can see us here. Just a little kiss!'

Roughly he pulled her towards him and planted his wet mouth upon her unwilling lips. She struggled against him, but Henry held her fast. She twisted her face away, but still his arms held her. She felt guilty, and disloyal to Guy, whom she loved, and yet there was guilt too in her secret affair with Guy Trent. Beside him Henry was rough and uncouth, yet he was sensitive enough to feel her revulsion. His arms locked about her more fiercely and his dark eyes searched her face in the shadowy half-light. 'We'll be married, Sarah, 'afore this year is out.'

Angrily, Sarah replied, 'That we won't, Henry Smithson!'

'And I say we *will!*' He made as if to kiss her again, but with one desperate push against him she fought herself free and ran from him, dodging between the trees, losing herself in the shadows.

'Sarah! Sarah! Come back!' Angrily Henry crashed his way through the undergrowth in search of her, but Sarah, hiding behind a bush, breathed a sigh of relief. He was going in the opposite direction.

A hand closed over her arm and Sarah gave a cry of fright, but turning she found herself looking into the laughing blue eyes of Guy Trent.

'Guy, oh Guy,' she breathed his name in a whisper of thankfulness and laid her head against his chest. His arms were about her, his lips against her dark hair.

‘Let’s escape from them,’ he murmured.

Hand in hand they slipped through the shadows, amongst the trees to where Guy had tethered his horse.

‘Tonight, you are mine and mine alone,’ he told her as he lifted her on to the horse and swung himself up behind her. In the moonlight they trotted out of the wood away from Abbeyford.

‘Guy, where are you taking me?’ Sarah gasped. ‘I must get back soon, or else I’ll be missed. Henry...’

Guy only laughed aloud and spurred his horse to a canter, his arm tightly around Sarah’s waist.

‘Oh lovely Sarah—we should run away, you and I, and never come back.’

Some distance away from Abbeyford, high on a hillside near a derelict shepherd’s hut, Guy pulled up and dismounted. He held up his arms to Sarah and she slid into them. Then, without warning, he picked her up in his arms and carried her towards the hut.

Inside it was surprisingly warm. Once more she made one feeble effort for reason, but his lips were upon hers silencing her protest. ‘Sarah, oh Sarah. Be mine, Sarah, be mine!’

His hands caressed her until, shivering with delight, she allowed him to unfasten her dress.

Reverently his eyes roamed over her nakedness bathed in soft moonlight.

'Oh you're lovely, lovely Sarah! I knew you would be.'

Her own hands ran through his hair, pulling his head down towards her and together they lay down. The tumbledown shack became their palace, the rough, makeshift bed their bower of love.

Softly she moaned his name like a prayer. 'Guy, oh Guy, my love.'

Willingly, lovingly, foolishly careless of the consequences, Sarah gave herself to him.

As the dawn crept palely into the shack, Sarah stirred and then sat bolt upright, terror-stricken. Beside her Guy lay sprawled in sleep, his arm flung carelessly across her.

'Guy—wake up!' She shook him and then fumbled to dress herself, to cover her nakedness—in the stark light of early morning sanity—her shame!

She began to sob and her fingers shook so that she could scarcely fasten the buttons of her dress.

'Oh what will they say? What will I do? Pa'll kill me!'

'Sarah?' Guy sat up, rubbing his eyes.

'Guy—Guy, take me back. No—you mustn't. Oh—I don't know what to do...' Her teeth were chattering with cold and fear.

'Sarah, Sarah, my love.' His hands held hers, warming her. 'Don't be afraid. I love you, Sarah.'

Still weeping, she shook her head muttering, 'I shouldn't have, oh I shouldn't have...'

'Sarah, look at me.' He cupped her chin and turned her face towards his. Her eyes, brimming with tears, met his steady gaze. 'I love you. I'll not let them harm you. I'll take you back to the Grange.'

'But I'm supposed to be at home—for Mayday.'

Guy sighed. 'Oh,' he said heavily. He thought for a moment. 'Couldn't you say you got separated from the others and—and went back to the Grange.'

Miserably she shook her head. 'From where we were—in the woods—it's further to the Grange than—than home.'

'But do your parents know exactly where you were?'

'Henry did.'

'Well—I still think you'd better say you've been at the Grange all night.'

'They'll not believe me,' she whispered.

They did not believe her. Later that afternoon, her knees trembling and her mouth dry, Sarah lifted the latch and let herself into the cottage.

Already the green was buzzing with the village folk on their days' freedom from work. The bright ribbons on the maypole fluttered gaily in the breeze. Laughter and jollity filled the air.

But in the tiny cottage Joseph Miller, home for the day's holiday, and his wife waited, grim-faced, for their daughter.

'Where were you last night?' Joseph demanded.

Sarah squared her shoulders and stuck to the story she had planned. 'At the Grange.' And added with an outward show of defiant haughtiness, 'Where else should I be?'

Joseph Miller and his wife exchanged a glance. 'How did you get back there? And why? I thought you were comin' home for the night?'

Sarah shrugged, but inwardly her stomach

churned. 'Lady Caroline needed me first thing this morning. I prepared her bath as usual and laid out her clothes. Ask her—if you don't believe me.'

Joseph made a sudden movement towards her as if to strike her but his wife's restraining hand was upon his arm.

'Wait. Sarah—is that the truth now? Were you at Abbeyford Grange last night?'

'I told you—I had to go back to help Lady Caroline.'

It was the truth—but not the whole truth. She had indeed returned to the Grange. Guy had taken her there, leaving her behind the stables. A fresh shiver of fear ran through her as she remembered how she had hidden there, waiting her moment to slip into the house, hiding again in the washhouse and then running stealthily through the main kitchen when the cook went into the pantry and the kitchen-maid bent over the range. Up the back stairs she had raced to the sanctuary of her own room, her heart thumping, her knees trembling. After a few moments to calm herself, she had changed her dress, splashed her face with cold water, tidied her hair and emerged as if she had spent the night in her room. She was fortunate none of the numerous servants had seen her return and lucky too to be back in time to appear at the usual hour to attend her mistress.

Now, holding her breath, she watched her parents look at each other. Joseph sighed and raised his shoulders in a weary shrug.

Mrs Miller's eyes were upon her daughter. 'Well then, we'll say na' more about it. You'd better go 'n join Henry. He's waitin'. He was worried to death last night. You'd better apologise to 'im.'

Sarah tossed her head, her confidence returning now that her story seemed to be believed. 'Huh! It's him that needs to apologise. His behaviour last night wasn't exactly perfect!'

Joseph started up again, 'What d'you mean...?'

But Sarah had gone, flinging open the cottage door and crashing it to behind her.

Ellen Miller sighed. 'What's to become of her I don't know.'

'I'm beginning to think perhaps Henry's right. She'd be better married to him—and soon!' Joseph growled.

Henry was sullen and Mayday quite

spoilt for them both.

'Why did you run off, Sarah?' he asked.

'You *know* why, Henry Smithson,' she said scornfully. 'We're not promised. You'd no right...'

He grasped her wrist. 'I've *every* right!'

'Let go—you're hurting me!'

'It's time you came to your senses. You can't have 'im, you know. He'll not *marry* you.'

'I—I don't know what you're talking about.'

Henry nodded grimly. 'I reckon you do. He's just amusing hissel'.'

Angrily Sarah twisted herself free. 'You dun't know anything about it, Henry Smithson, so hold your tongue!'

Sourly Henry watched her go.

CHAPTER 8

Although there was no one amongst the village labourers who would dare tell Lord Royston of his daughter's secret meetings with Thomas Cole—and they had all known for some time—there was one person who was not afraid, indeed was gleeful to have the opportunity for personal spite against her envied cousin.

Word of Caroline's affair had come to the ears of Martha Langley!

Two days after Mayday Martha Langley walked up the lane towards Abbeyford Grange, determination in every stride.

She stood before Lord Royston in his book-lined library, her hands folded in front of her, her lips pursed to their customary thinness.

'I thought you should know, my lord, I thought it my duty to tell you—for her own sake—that Caroline is meeting frequently with the Trents' bailiff, Thomas Cole. Far too often for it to be a mere casual acquaintanceship.'

Lord Royston glared at her, but, not in the least deterred, Martha stared back at him.

Lord Royston prided himself on being a good judge of character. He had never liked Martha Langley or her mother, his late wife's sister. Early on in their marriage he had detected the jealousy in Martha's mother, who had been unable to make as good a marriage as her sister. That jealousy had been bred into Martha and she directed it at her wealthier, more beautiful cousin, Caroline. Nevertheless her malicious gossip was disturbing. He was also uncomfortably aware of the wilful nature, the strength of character, of his own daughter and had known that when she grew to womanhood he would have to find the right suitor for her quickly lest she choose for herself someone entirely unsuitable. Without his wife to guide him he had failed to realise that at nineteen his daughter was already a woman grown.

He had left it too late!

With a growl of anger, directed not only against himself for his tardiness but against Martha Langley for being the bearer of such ill news, he said grudgingly, 'Yes—I should be told.' But he could not bring himself to express words of thanks to her!

Lord Royston decided his best approach was not to confront his daughter about her meetings with Thomas Cole, not even to let her know that he knew of them. Instead he would whisk her away to London, give her a generous allowance to spend freely on all the things women loved: new clothes, jewellery—anything she wanted.

The season did not end until the

beginning of June—time enough left for a busy round of routs, balls and parties to obliterate all fanciful thoughts of Thomas Cole. Indeed there might even be some eligible viscount ready to offer his hand, if Lord Royston let it be known in society circles that Caroline was the sole heiress to his estate.

He would prise her away from Thomas Cole without her realising what was happening.

But Lord Royston had misjudged the strength of his daughter's will and miscalculated the extent to which the affair had already gone. By pretending no knowledge of it, he allowed Caroline to believe herself undiscovered.

She agreed quite readily to go to London, even though being parted from Thomas for even a short while caused her pain. She anticipated a few weeks in society happily, ignorant of the scheming which lay behind the proposal. She did not even suspect when she found herself accompanied wherever she went, either by her father himself or by one of his servants appointed to accompany her, so that clandestine meetings with Thomas became impossible. She thought it coincidence and her only worry was that she was obliged to leave for London without having seen him, without having had chance to explain the reasons why she had not met him recently.

In desperation she had taken Sarah into her confidence. Her maid had listened wide-eyed whilst Caroline had pressed a letter into her hand.

'Now listen carefully, Sarah. This afternoon is your half-day off, is it not?'

The girl had nodded.

'Good. Then I want you to deliver this note to Thomas Cole, who lives in the cottage next to the wheelwright. You know where I mean, don't you?'

Again Sarah had nodded, dumb with amazement that Lady Caroline should be sending letters to an estate worker. Perhaps, she thought, her mind clinging to any excuse, it is a letter about estate matters, but Caroline herself dispelled this illusion with her next words.

'You must not let this letter fall into anyone else's hands. You understand? No one must even know about it, let alone see it.'

'Yes, m'lady.'

But Caroline's plans were thwarted, not,

this time, by her own father, but by Sarah's father who met her from the Grange and accompanied her back there the same evening. Sarah dared not deliver the letter in her father's presence. In his present ever-suspicious mood he would be sure to question her closely.

Sarah was almost in tears the following morning as, with trembling fingers, she held out the letter to her mistress.

'I couldna take it, m'lady. Me pa was with me all the time.'

Caroline snatched the letter from her and snapped, 'Oh you useless girl! Get out of my sight! Can you not even deliver a letter for me? I've a good mind not to take you to London with me!'

Sarah crept from the room. It was the first time Lady Caroline had spoken so sharply to her.

So Caroline had to leave Abbeyford without having been able to send Thomas any explanation, but she was sure he would be there, still waiting for her when she returned to Abbeyford.

Thomas Cole, when he heard of her departure, sadly thought she had grown tired of him, as he had believed she would eventually. Though he had warned himself to expect it, her sudden seeming rejection of him cut deeply, wounded him and tore away his happiness.

Thomas Cole began to think of leaving Abbeyford, of seeking a new life in America, as far away from Caroline as he could get!

Caroline did not carry out her threat to leave her maid behind, though Sarah almost wished she had. Once she would have been excited by the visit to the big city, but now, now she had met Guy and she could not bear to leave him. Miserably she imagined that as soon as she was away from him Guy would swiftly forget her and amuse himself with another village girl. Or worse, he would marry one of his own kind and be lost to her for ever!

It was quite an entourage that set out for London, for Lord Royston, whilst accompanying his daughter himself, felt the need of advice and help from his dear friend Lady Lynwood, and he had prevailed upon her to go with them.

'I have to take you into my confidence, my dear Elizabeth. Caroline is consorting with my estate's bailiff!' Lord Royston marched the length of Lady Lynwood's morning-room whilst she watched him from her sofa. As he turned to walk back towards her, she nodded and said, 'I didn't know, but I cannot say that I am surprised. I noticed on the day of the hunt that her eyes continually sought out a young man who was unknown to me. I wondered then—partly because of my own son's reactions. He is excessively fond of Caroline, you know.'

Lord Royston agreed. ' 'Tis a great pity he is not a little older—I would have willingly arranged a marriage between them. Of course,' he shrugged, 'four years is no age difference to speak of, once Francis reaches maturity. But, Elizabeth, I dare not wait that long. Caroline is a wilful, headstrong girl and I—I fear the consequences of further delay. Already it seems I have waited too long.'

'So what do you propose to do?'

'Take her to London. There are still some six weeks of the season left.'

'And you hope that in that time she will forget this bailiff?'

'I'm convinced she will. Once amongst her own kind, she will see her own folly. Here she has no company of her own class of her own age. Elizabeth—will you come with us? Please? I ask you as an old and valued friend. Now Adeline is gone—I...' He passed his hand wearily across his forehead. 'I hardly know what to do for the best.'

Lady Lynwood smiled. 'Think no more of it, Robert. We shall leave for London as soon as we can be ready. And Francis shall come too. Although he is still a trifle young for society life, he looks older than his years and perhaps if he were to have the chance to see other delectable young ladies in society, maybe it would help him to overcome his obsession with Caroline. Perhaps we can help both our children at the same time.'

Lord Royston looked at her in surprise. 'I had realised he was extremely fond of Caroline, but is it really so deep?'

Soberly, Lady Lynwood nodded. 'I fear so, Robert. I am afraid his feelings for her are much too deep for his own good.' A wistfulness came into her eyes. 'And, if he is anything like his father, then those emotions will be difficult to change. It will take an exceptional girl to make him forget Caroline!'

Lord Royston turned away, a little embarrassed. He knew a little of his old friend's romantic love-affair with Elizabeth—how he had married her against his parents' wishes, who had objected to her birth and background. Yet their marriage had been superbly happy and Elizabeth had proved herself to be far more of a 'lady' than many born to that position. He had pondered on the wisdom of confiding in her—knowing of her own story—and yet there was no one else to whom he could turn.

So they set out for London in three carriages—Lady Lynwood, Lord Royston, Caroline and Francis in one, their servants in a second and the third was piled high with their trunks and boxes.

Sarah Miller found the city life totally different from anything she could have imagined.

The roads, as they neared London, were thronged with coaches and carriages and riders on horseback. The country girl who had never even visited a large town, let alone a city, was appalled by the narrow crowded streets, the bustle and noise, the cries of the street-merchants, the dirty ragged urchins begging for money, or picking pockets when they could.

She shuddered and longed for the

tranquillity of the country. She grew pale and wan and was physically sick with longing to return to the familiar surroundings—and people—of Abbeyford valley.

She was afraid of the servants at Lord Royston's town house in London. They ridiculed her strange way of talking—though to Sarah their speech was just as peculiar. They laughed at her coarse dress and heavy clogs.

But Lady Caroline blossomed in the different environment, though she too, in her innermost heart, longed to return to Abbeyford and to Thomas—and she was determined that before very long she would do so!

It took Sarah some time to become accustomed to the new and strange routine. Lady Caroline now rose very late in the morning. After a light breakfast she would make social calls with Lady Lynwood or visit the dressmakers and milliners. Dinner was in the early evening and then she would dance until the early hours of the following day.

The weeks passed during which, young though he was, Lynwood accompanied his mother and Lady Caroline to many of the functions and he was obliged to stand and watch with envious eyes whilst Caroline danced and flirted with every dandy in sight. One Viscount Grosmore paid her particular attention and soon he was Caroline's constant escort.

One evening, when attending a very important ball where many influential people would be present, Caroline decided to follow the daring new fashion which was all the rage in revolutionary France. She instructed Sarah to dress her hair very simply in the style of Ancient Greece, with curls at the back of her head held in place with a ribbon.

As she laid out the new gown only delivered from the dressmaker that morning, Sarah gasped in horror. It was a straight gown, girdled just below the bosom, but what shocked the country girl was the low-cut of the neckline, the short, puffed sleeves and the transparency of the material. After being accustomed to the full-skirted heavy silk ball-gowns Lady Caroline had worn until this moment, Sarah held up the diaphanous garment in perplexity.

'M'lady, has there been some mistake? Is—is this an under-garment?'

Caroline turned from the mirror. 'No—

you silly goose. *This* is the petticoat.' Caroline giggled and her eyes held mischief. 'I want you to dampen it slightly for me, Sarah, just the skirt part.'

Sarah's violet eyes were still puzzled. 'Whatever for, m'lady?'

'You'll see. Just do as I say.'

By the time Caroline was dressed, Sarah was even more shocked and by now really anxious. 'Oh m'lady, I don't think your papa will—will approve.'

The dampened petticoat clung to Caroline's body, emphasising her shapeliness, barely concealed by the transparent gown over it.

Caroline tossed her head and her eyes glinted. '*He* brought me to London. He must want me to involve myself with society and all its ways,' she said defiantly and added, 'if he doesn't like it, then perhaps we shall return to Abbeyford all the sooner.'

Sarah watched her go, her long cloak covering the daring gown. Perhaps, Sarah thought shrewdly, it was Caroline's way of getting what she wanted. Sighing, Sarah began folding all her mistress's discarded clothing and tidying the bedroom. She would then snatch a few hours sleep before she would have to awake in readiness for Caroline's return.

But Sarah was awakened suddenly by the early return of her mistress who fell on to her bed, her face buried in the pillow, her whole body shaking.

Caroline had concealed her gown from Lady Lynwood, her father and Francis until their arrival at the ball. As she removed her cloak in the room set aside for the ladies, she heard Lady Lynwood's gasp and turned to see her staring almost open-mouthed at Caroline's gown.

'My dear—whatever is that?'

'Why, Lady Lynwood, this is the latest fashion. Don't tell me you have not observed that this is what all the ladies of fashion are wearing. Why, only last evening...'

Lady Lynwood felt the laughter bubbling up inside her. The little minx! she thought, but could not help being more amused than angry at the girl's daring. It was so like the sort of thing she herself would have done at the same age, she had to admit.

With a great effort Lady Lynwood retained a straight face; indeed for the sake of her dear friend, Lord Royston, she attempted to adopt an expression of severe displeasure. 'I doubt your father will appreciate your—er—devotion to fashion, my dear. I think it would be wisest if you were to return to the house and put on something a little less—er—revealing.'

'I shall do no such thing,' Caroline retorted and she repeated the words she had spoken to Sarah. 'Since it was Papa's idea for me to come to London—I'm sure he must want me to participate fully in the ways of society.' She slanted her green eyes, full of mischievous cunning, at Lady Lynwood, but this time she added nothing about returning home to Abbeyford. Without waiting for any reply, Caroline left the room and made a grand entrance into the ballroom.

Her arrival caused little stir amongst those who did not know her family well, but Lord Royston and those of his acquaintance were appalled by her appearance.

Lady Lynwood, entering a moment after Caroline, saw Lord Royston marching purposefully across the room towards his daughter.

Young Lynwood watched, his eyes unfathomable depths.

'What is the meaning of this, Caroline?' her father thundered, quite oblivious to the whispers and mocking smiles of those nearby.

Caroline turned innocent eyes upon her father. 'Why, Papa, 'tis the latest rage, have you not noticed...?'

'How dare you appear in such—unseemly attire? Leave at once, do you hear me?'

'My Lord Royston, pray forgive my intrusion...' Lord Grosmore began, but Lord Royston turned on him in fury.

'This is no concern of yours, Grosmore, you'll oblige me...'

'I was about to offer my carriage to convey Lady Caroline—and of course Lady Lynwood—home, where she may change and return...'

'We have our own carriage, Grosmore,' he muttered gruffly, 'and my daughter will most certainly not return here tonight—nor for that matter any other night. We shall be returning to the country.'

'Oh my Lord Royston,' Lord Grosmore bowed ingratiatingly, 'I had no wish to offend you. Pray believe me...?'

Lord Royston dismissed him with a wave of his hand, took hold of his daughter by the elbow and propelled her from the ballroom. Lady Lynwood and her son followed.

So it was that Lady Caroline arrived home in a great flurry to be found on her bed by Sarah.

The girl touched her mistress lightly on the shoulder. 'Oh, m'lady.'

Caroline rolled over on to her back and Sarah was astounded to see that she was rocking with laughter!

'It worked—oh Sarah, it worked! We are to return to Abbeyford tomorrow!'

Sarah wept with relief.

'Sarah—what has happened to you, child? Are you ill?' Ellen Miller spread her arms wide and enfolded her daughter to her bosom. Then she held her back at arm's length and looked critically into her face.

'No, Ma—well...I dun't like the city, Ma.' Tears welled in her eyes. 'I were that homesick.'

'Well, dun't fret no more. You're home now. Beth—welcome your sister home. Let her warm hersel' by the fire.'

Beth moved forward reluctantly. 'Wish I'd been given the chance to go to London. You dun't know how lucky you are, our Sarah.'

Huddling near the fire, cold and shivering after the days of travelling over rough and dangerous roads, Sarah didn't feel at all lucky. She was thankful to be home, back in Abbeyford, back with her family. And soon—she might see Guy!

Somewhere in the pit of her stomach she felt a fluttery feeling of excitement at the thought of seeing him again.

'We'll soon have you rosy-cheeked 'n blooming again, our Sarah,' Ellen Miller smiled. 'Dun't you fret.'

On the same day that Sarah returned from London, late at night a weary Joseph Miller walked down the hill from Amberly towards Abbeyford village. He paused on the footbridge near the ford.

Clearly in the moonlight he could see the lines of fencing criss-crossing the common land.

Without giving conscious thought to what he meant to do, he walked slowly towards where the fencing started. He stood a moment, just looking at it. Then he pushed at one of the posts. Newly erected, the post moved in the soft earth and almost before he had realised what he was doing Joseph had pulled up the post and flung it away as far as he could. He moved on to the next upright and began to pull at that too.

Anger and resentment gave him strength and soon much of the new fencing lay scattered on the ground. He uprooted the young saplings which had been planted at intervals along the fencing and with his heavy boots he crushed the young roots.

Breathing hard, Joseph stood in the bright moonlight and surveyed the havoc he had wrought single-handed. Never in his life before had he committed an act of destruction on something that was now someone else's property. But his rage against Sir Matthew for robbing him of his rights on the waste-land, and now too his anger against Guy for turning Sarah's head, had temporarily robbed him of his sanity.

Joseph Miller retraced his steps across the footbridge and returned up the hill out of Abbeyford.

He did not want to be in the village when the damage was discovered the following morning.

'Have you any idea who could have done it?' Sir Matthew demanded of Thomas

Cole who had brought him the news of the destruction of the fencing.

'No, sir.'

'Hmm.' Sir Matthew grunted and added brusquely, 'Find out where Miller was last night.'

'Joseph Miller?' Thomas's surprise showed in his voice. 'I don't think he would commit such a crime, Sir Matthew.'

'He harbours resentment against the enclosure of the common land.'

'Yes—I know, but...'

'Don't argue, man. Do as I say!'

Thomas Cole, as parish constable as well as bailiff, made enquiries throughout the village, but all he could learn was that Joseph Miller had been away from Abbeyford to find work and had not been home on the night the damage had been done.

Sir Matthew received the news with scepticism. 'Well, on this occasion we can prove nothing, but I still think it was Miller. There's no one else who would dare!'

A week later Joseph returned home and feigned surprise when Ellen told him of the damage done to the new fences.

'Mr Cole came askin' about you, Joseph, but I told him as how you was away seeking work.'

'Aye, you did right,' was all Joseph would say.

The fences were repaired and more saplings planted and this time they were not touched!

The days passed after Caroline returned home from London and still she had no chance of meeting Thomas. Always there seemed to be someone near, someone watching her every move. Late one night, when she believed everyone at the Grange to be asleep, Caroline slipped from her warm bed and dressed. She stole along the moonlit landings. The shadowy portraits of her ancestors seemed to look down upon her with disapproval.

Out of the side door, Caroline made her way to the stables where, with much tugging and heaving, she managed to saddle her horse. She was accustomed to having such menial tasks done for her. Nor did it occur to Lady Caroline to *walk* to the village to see Thomas!

Leaving her horse tethered near the stone bridge, her heart beating fast, she hurried past the smithy and the wheelwright's cottage. The cottage next to that had a soft light shining out from the ill-fitting curtains.

Caroline crept forward and to her relief saw Thomas seated at the table, bending forward as if he were writing something, his brown wavy hair almost touching the lighted candle on the table. Her heart turned over at the sight of him. She knocked on the door and when it opened she flung herself against him, almost knocking him over.

'Thomas, Thomas! How I've missed you. My father sent me to London and I couldn't get word to you, couldn't see you. Oh I was so afraid you would think the worst...'

'Caroline, Caroline.' Gently he eased himself from her clinging arms and closed the door.

'Oh Thomas, it wasn't my fault. You must believe me. Say you believe me? Say you still love me, as I love you, darling Thomas?'

Wistfully, Thomas hushed her near-hysteria. 'My dearest Caroline, I still love you. I shall always love you. But,' he sighed, 'these weeks have shown me that—that our love can never be.'

'Why?' she cried passionately.

'My darling, your father must have heard something about our meetings. If not everything, then enough to make him suspicious. Enough to make him take you away from Abbeyford for a time.'

Caroline gasped. 'You really think so?'

'Yes, my love, I do. You must realise that he—he will never allow anything to—to come of it.'

Defiantly Caroline tossed her head. 'Then we must run away. For I declare I won't marry Lord Grosmore. He's a conceited dandy and I hate him!'

Already Thomas had heard the village gossip concerning Grosmore who had become a frequent visitor to the Grange ever since Caroline's return from London.

'My darling—he is of your world and I—I am not.'

'Thomas! Don't say such things.' She wound her arms about him. 'I will *not* marry Lord Grosmore—and I shall marry you.'

Thomas drew her close, desperately savouring every moment he could hold her in his arms, knowing that their love could never be, that it would be wrong of him to take her away from the only life she knew—a life of comfort and luxury and security.

Caroline threw back her head and gazed up into his eyes. 'We must go on seeing each other, but we'll have to be very careful, that's all.'

But Caroline was not careful. Indeed she was very thoughtless.

Whilst she slept late the following morning, Lord Royston found her horse in the stable, still saddled and caked with mud. Angered by her ill-treatment of an animal, he also guessed that his wayward daughter had resumed her meetings with Thomas Cole. And at night too! It was unthinkable.

Lord Royston returned to the house, rage in every stride.

His loud voice rang through the hall. 'Fetch Lady Caroline to me at once!'

Mrs Hargreaves appeared, flustered and anxious at the anger in Lord Royston's tone. 'She—she's still sleeping m'lord.'

'Then wake her, woman, wake her!' his lordship roared. He flung open the double doors into the morning-room where he paced the floor until Caroline appeared, her eyes heavy with sleep, her rich auburn hair in tangled disarray.

'What is it, Papa?'

'Come in and close the door behind you,' her father said grimly as he stood with his back to the fire, facing her.

She did as he bade and then came to stand before him. As she saw the fury in his eyes, even Caroline's resolute heart faltered and for the first time in her young life she feared her father's wrath. He began to speak slowly, as if weighing each word deliberately before it was spoken. 'I would have preferred not to speak of this matter to you—but it seems I must.'

'Papa, I...'

'Be quiet, I have not finished. You have disgraced yourself. The whole village knows of your—your liaison with Cole. You will not see him again. You will not leave this house unaccompanied and at night, since you obviously cannot be trusted, your bedroom door will be locked.'

'Papa!' Caroline cried in anguish and flung herself against him, crying. 'But, Papa—I love him. And he loves me!'

'What do you know of *love?* And as for him—he's nothing better than a fortune-hunter.'

'That's not true?' Angrily Caroline stood back from him. Tears shimmering in her eyes, she faced her father defiantly. 'I wanted to tell you myself, but he said you wouldn't understand, he said...' she faltered, reluctant to repeat exactly what Thomas had said—that Lord Royston would dismiss him and send him away from Abbeyford, in case her father should pounce on that very idea as a solution.

'Well, at least he seems to have shown a little sense there,' Lord Royston murmured.

'But I told him you would only want my happiness, that you could not possibly be so—cruel as to...'

Lord Royston gave a wry laugh. 'Really, my child, don't you realise the foolishness of your conduct? Did you ever *really* suppose anything could come of it? My estate bailiff!'

Caroline tossed her head. 'I don't care. I would still love him if he were a—a beggar!'

Lord Royston's eyes glinted. He leant towards her and said slowly and deliberately, 'Would you indeed, my dear?'

Caroline drew her breath swiftly in horror at the implied threat in his tone.

'Oh Papa—you wouldn't. You *couldn't!*'

'Oh couldn't I?'

Caroline turned and fled from the room in tears. Lord Royston watched her go, his anger giving way to sorrow now. Of course he wanted his daughter to be happy, but not for one moment could he countenance Caroline marrying the estate bailiff!

CHAPTER 9

Sarah's paleness and sickness did not disappear even after she had been home a few weeks. The rosiness was gone from her cheeks and beneath her once-bright eyes were dark shadows.

'Oh Sarah, my lovely Sarah—what have they done to you?'

She was in his arms again. Guy had not forgotten her.

Her reply was muffled against his chest. 'I didn't like the city, Guy, and—I missed you so.'

He stroked her black hair. 'Oh Sarah. Listen, you must not meet me for a while at night, not until...'

She looked up into his face, her violet eyes wide and fearful, her heart hammering. 'Why—why not?'

'You must get yourself well again.'

'I am well. Please Guy—don't say that...' She wound her arms around him. 'Please don't. Let me see you!' she begged.

'I'm only thinking of you. I want to see you too, but...'

'Do you? Do you really?I was so afraid you would have forgotten me.'

'Sarah, oh my Sarah!' His mouth came down hard upon hers and she allowed herself to be consumed in the fire of his passion.

So their nightly meetings began again and Sarah grew more pale and listless and exhaustd for she still had to be up early to do her work as usual.

On one of her Sunday visits to the cottage in the village Mrs Miller asked, 'Are you ill, child? I'd hoped to see you better by now. That city were no good for you, but I thought once you'd been home a bit...'

Three pairs of eyes turned upon Sarah—only Ella, sitting in her usual corner, took no notice.

'I'm a bit tired and—I keep being sick.

Must be the rich food up at the Grange.'

Her mother bridled. 'I'm sure I don't know what you mean. You've always been well-fed at home.'

'How long have you been feeling badly?' Her father's question was sharp.

'A couple of weeks or—or so.'

'How long—*exactly?*'

Her voice was a whisper. 'Nearly six weeks.'

Her father moved suddenly and came to stand over her. He gripped her chin with his strong fingers and forced her head back till her neck hurt.

'Look at me! Have you been a bad girl while you've been in London, Sarah?'

'No—no—I...'

'The truth!' he thundered. 'You've lied before—remember?'

Sarah closed her eyes. She felt him release her, felt the draught of air as he drew back his hand. Then he hit her twice, once on each side of the face, with such force that she was knocked first one way and then the other.

'You're with child, aren't you? *Aren't you?*'

'No—no,' she screamed from the floor where she had fallen, but now he grabbed hold of her arms and hauled her to her feet. He shook her like a limp rag-doll.

Her mother looked on, making no attempt to interfere this time. Beth smiled smugly.

'Who is it? Who's—the father? Someone in London?'

Dumbly Sarah shook her head.

'Who then? *Who?* Not—not *Henry?*'

Again Sarah shook her head, this time even more vehemently.

'I know,' piped up Beth. 'It's him, isn't it, our Sarah? It's Guy Trent.'

'Oh my God!' groaned Joseph Miller. 'I thought we'd put a stop to *that!*'

'Oh I've seen 'em,' Beth continued gleefully. 'Meetin' in the woods or the ruins. An' I'll tell you some'at else an' all. Me Lady Caroline'll be ending up the same way as our Sarah, if she dun't watch out, with that Thomas Cole.'

'Hold your tongue, girl,' her father growled. 'That's no concern of ourn, but this'n is!'

Again he shook Sarah savagely and then flung her away from him in disgust and stormed out of the cottage slamming the door behind him.

Sarah crumpled into a sorry heap upon the floor.

'Oh Sarah. How could you?' her mother mourned. 'How *could* you?'

'What'll happen?' Beth asked pertly, seeming to enjoy the situation, though Ella, sitting in the corner rocking her doll, said not a word. Much of what was happening passed completely over her head, did not penetrate her private little world.

''Cos he won't marry her!' Beth continued. 'They're arranging for him to marry a girl from Manchester way. Louisa somebody.'

Sarah raised her tear-streaked face to look at her sister. 'What? What did you say?'

'I'm friends with Mary Tuplin, aren't I?' Beth retorted cockily, 'and Mary Tuplin's Lady Trent's maid, ain't she? An' she overhears things, doesn't she?'

Sarah's tears flowed afresh. So, all his sweet words, all his promises, had been idle flattery to make her give herself to him.

Sarah bowed her head in shame.

Joseph Miller did not return home until the early hours of the following morning.

'Where is she?' he demanded of his wife as he flung open the door of the bedroom they shared. Ellen Miller, awakened from her sleep, sat up, bleary eyed and startled. 'Oh Joseph, what a fright you gave me! Where have you been?'

'Where's Sarah?' he asked again, ignoring his wife's question.

'She—she's gone back to the Grange.'

'God in Heaven, woman! You let her go?'

Ellen flinched in the face of his wrath. Her man was rarely moved to violent anger but when he was he was fearsome. He slammed the door behind him making the whole cottage shake. Grumbling to himself he began to take off his boots. Ellen lay back and let her eyes close, seeking the oblivion of sleep once more. But she was aroused again by her husband's voice.

'She's to be brought home. Henry'll have her. I've fixed it all. They're to be married quick.'

Ellen was silent. It would be for the best, she told herself, but knowing Henry's nature she could not predict a happy future for her daughter as his wife.

Joseph Miller went to Abbeyford Grange the very next morning and explained the situation to Lady Caroline in person. He did not spare Sarah, nor himself, in telling her the full story of their family's shame. Later Caroline faced Sarah.

'Oh Sarah, you're a fool. Why—why did you let yourself be taken in by him?'

Fresh tears spilled over on to cheeks already puffed from a night's weeping. Dumbly she shook her head.

Caroline sighed. 'You know he's a rogue, don't you? You were a plaything to him.'

Lady Caroline was confirming Sarah's worst fears, fuelling the doubts against him which her family had already put into her mind.

'You cannot possibly have thought he would—or could *marry* you?' Caroline's tone was incredulous that such a thought might ever have been entertained by a girl of Sarah's birth. Caroline, in her blind selfishness, could not see that she herself was treading on as equally dangerous ground as Sarah, in her affair with Thomas Cole.

Sarah gulped. 'He—he said—he loved me.' But the words spoken aloud in a last desperate effort, sounded unconvincing even to Sarah's own ears.

In the harsh light of day, and in the face of cruel reality, Guy's murmured words of love seemed only a lovely dream.

Lady Caroline sighed. 'Your father tells me you are to marry your cousin Henry.'

Sarah nodded.

'Then you had better pack your things and leave today,' Caroline said coldly, all trace of the friendliness she had previously shown her maid gone in an instant. Dejectedly Sarah left the room. Caroline clicked with exasperation. She was angry with Sarah, not so much for the girl's sake but for her own selfish reasons. With Sarah gone, how could she send messages to Thomas?

Lord Royston had carried out his threat. Caroline was never alone and at night her bedroom door was locked. The only way she had been able to keep contact with Thomas Cole had been to send notes to him through Sarah.

Never once, though, had Thomas replied and although Sarah had repeatedly assured her mistress that Thomas was still here in Abbeyford, still employed as the bailiff, Caroline was so afraid that suddenly he would leave either by his own choice or on dismissal by her father and she would lose him.

And now even that link with her lover was broken.

'Damn Sarah Miller!' Caroline muttered crossly, her concern solely for herself. Not one moments' thought did she spare for the unhappy Sarah and the life of misery that lay before her.

Sarah carried her bag down the lane away from Abbeyford Grange, reluctantly returning to the cottage in the village. She came to the place where the trees overhung the lane. She heard the hoofbeats behind her and his voice calling urgently, 'Sarah! Sarah!'

Her heart gave a leap, but she continued walking, head bowed. Guy drew level with her and flung himself from his horse. *'Sarah!'*

Still she did not stop to look up.

He caught her by the shoulders and spun her round, almost throwing her off balance. His eyes were wild.

'Why, Sarah? Why?' Torment was in his voice.

So—he had heard already! Heard she was to be made to marry Henry Smithson.

'Look at me, Sarah!'

Slowly she raised her eyes and looked into his face and her heart turned over. She loved him still. Wild, reckless, irresponsible—wicked, some would say—though he was, she would always love him.

'I must. It's all arranged,' she said flatly.

'But—but *why?*'

She hung her head and murmured almost inaudibly, 'I'm with child.'

He was motionless. For a moment he seemed to stop breathing. Then harshly he asked, 'His?'

Her head snapped up, her dark eyes wide. 'No—oh no!'

His anger softened. 'Mine?'

She nodded and allowed him to draw her towards him, her head against his chest, his chin resting on her dark hair.

'You *can't* marry Smithson, Sarah—we'll be married. I love you. I told you that! Didn't you believe me?'

'They—they said you didn't mean it. Even Lady Caroline said you wouldn't marry the likes of me.'

'Well, we'll see about that!' Guy said firmly. 'Just trust me, Sarah. Trust me!'

He held her close, fiercely protective, and she melted against him.

Without his strength, she was lost, lonely and afraid. But as soon as she was once more in his embrace, everything seemed to come right.

'Never!' Sir Matthew Trent shouted, his face purple with rage. 'A common village slut and you want to *marry* her? And a *Miller* too.'

Guy Trent faced his parents squarely: his father's anger and his mother's tears, as she lay back upon a sofa almost at the point of fainting.

'Yes—I do. I love her and she loves me.'

'Pah! Love! What has that got to do with it?' Sir Matthew bellowed. He prodded his forefinger towards his son. 'You'll marry Louisa Marchant, boy, and be glad her father's willing that you should!'

'I shall not. I shall marry Sarah.'

'You—will—not!' roared his father. 'You're a disgrace to the name of Trent. I'll arrange for the girl to be sent away to have it.' Grimly he added, 'She's not the first to bear your bastard, is she? But, by God, she'd better be the last!'

'This time it's different. The other two—well—they were nothing to me. But Sarah...'

'Have you no *shame*, boy? You dare to stand there and admit you've wronged three young girls and yet you show no remorse, no feeling...'

'I *do* care—about Sarah,' Guy shouted heatedly. 'Not about the other two—I admit. Besides, they weren't virgins...'

Lady Trent gave a little cry and her head lolled back.

'Hold your vulgar tongue, boy, in front of your mother.'

But Guy ignored his warning. 'But Sarah was. She belongs to me and only to me. I won't have her married to Smithson.'

'What? What's that?'

Sullenly Guy explained. 'Her father's arranged that she should marry Henry Smithson.'

'Smithson—my cowman?'

'Yes.'

Sir Matthew's anger subsided and he almost beamed to realise the problem had already been half-solved for him by the girl's father.

'There you are then. That's the answer to everything. I'll see young Smithson right. They must be given a cottage and...'

'No—no—*no!*' Guy yelled. He turned and almost ran from the room. 'I won't let her marry him—I *won't!*'

The door slammed behind him, rattling Lady Trent's fine china in its cabinet. Sir Matthew sank into a chair and exchanged a look of sheer defeat and helplessness with his wife.

Guy Trent hammered on the door of the Millers' cottage.

'Sarah! Are you in there, Sarah! I want to talk to you.' Again he thumped on the door with his clenched fist.

The door was flung open and Guy almost hit Joseph Miller in the face as he raised his hand to strike the door again.

'Good-day, Mr Trent.' Joseph's face was a grim mask.

Guy was panting hard for he had galloped, angry and distraught, from the Manor after the heated exchange with his father.

'I want to see Sarah.'

'Sarah is—not available.'

'She is—to me!' Guy made as if to enter the cottage by force, but Joseph's strong arm against the door frame stopped him.

'Mr Trent—we'll settle this trouble ourselves, if you dun't mind.'

'I've a right to see her.'

Joseph shook his head. 'My daughter is to marry Henry Smithson.'

'Sarah! *Sarah!*' Guy shouted and thought he caught the sound of muffled sobbing from within the cottage.

'Let me in!' He caught hold of Joseph's arm but the older man was bigger, tougher, stronger even than Guy Trent.

'Mr Trent,' Joseph said yet again, his patience ready to snap, 'I don't want to quarrel with you, and God knows I've just cause, but I've me home and family to think of.' He held the younger man easily at arm's length and, though fit and strong, Guy Trent was no match for the burly farm-labourer.

'You've brought shame to this family and me and mine'll not forgive you.'

'Miller, listen to me. I love Sarah. I want to marry her. Please...'

Joseph Miller shook his head. 'Your sort don't marry the likes of us, Mr Trent. You know that,' and added bitterly, 'you'll use our young lasses for your pleasure, but when it comes to marrying,' he gave a bark of wry laughter, 'you'll marry your own kind.'

'I must see her, talk to her,' Guy persisted.

'She dun't want to see you. She's agreed to marry young Smithson.'

Guy closed his eyes and groaned and his hands fell away from Joseph's arm. As he felt the younger man give way, Joseph relaxed his hold. Even he was surprised by the look of utter misery on Guy Trent's face. Perhaps he did care for Sarah—but no, marriage between them was out of the question. They were trapped by the accident of birth which separated their lives.

As Guy turned away, defeated on all sides, Joseph was moved to add, 'Sarah'll be all right. I'll see to that.'

They were all against him. The whole village were ranged behind the Miller family against Guy Trent. Even his own parents. He didn't even catch a glimpse of Sarah, let alone have a chance to talk to her.

If only they had let him see her, he could have persuaded her to run away with him. He knew he could! Perhaps that was the very thing they were afraid would happen.

As it was, the days slipped past towards her wedding-day.

Guy made one last desperate effort to see her. He went again to the Millers' cottage and was met at the door this time by both Joseph Miller and Henry Smithson. They would not listen to his arguments. Henry stood clenching and unclenching his fists, conscious of the desire to knock Guy Trent to the ground, to beat his face to an unrecognisable pulp, to kill him!

Already it was growing dusk as Guy Trent turned away from the Millers' cottage and flung himself on to his horse and turned, not westwards towards the Manor but across the common and up the hill out of the valley. Away from Abbeyford—he had to get away from Abbeyford; from the Millers, from his parents—away from everyone who stood between him and Sarah.

Henry Smithson watched him go, resentment festering in his heart. Quietly he too left the Millers' cottage, walked up the lane and across the footbridge near the ford and on up the hill, taking the right-hand fork which led to Amberly.

Although Guy Trent had galloped off in his frenzy towards the north, shrewdly Henry guessed that in his present mood he would seek the solace of drink. But he would not return to the Monk's Arms in Abbeyford—not this night. The most likely place he would go eventually would be the inn at Amberly and, if so, then Guy Trent would return home by this route.

Silently Henry Smithson slipped into the shadows of the wood and there he lay in wait for Guy Trent.

Darkness came completely, but anger and hatred kept Henry Smithson oblivious to the cold, the damp and even his own bodily weariness after a day's work in the fields. One thought filled his mind.

Guy Trent! He would kill Guy Trent!

Hour after hour he lay in wait. The eeriness of the woodland by night held no fears for him; he scarcely heard the rustling undergrowth, the hooting owls, nor the incessant waterfall. His ears strained for only one sound—the sound of hoofbeats from the direction of Amberly.

In the early hours of the morning Henry moved stiffly, stamped his feet and then listened. Faintly, growing louder with each moment, came the sound for which he had waited through the long cold hours.

He slipped off his jacket and crouched low behind a bush at the side of the track through the wood as nearer and nearer came the steady rhythmic cantering hooves.

Louder and louder, nearer and nearer.

Henry leapt from his hiding-place, flapping his coat and yelling. The horse whinnied and shied, rearing up above Henry, but he dodged to one side. The rider toppled from its back and the terrified animal bolted.

Henry stood over the motionless form on the ground, bent down and grasped him by his clothes. Twice as strong, Henry Smithson hauled him to his feet and without even giving Guy Trent time to recover his senses, to defend himself, he smashed his fist into his young master's face.

'Take my Sarah, would you?' Henry was weeping with rage, each blow punctuated by a verbal insult. 'You pig! You—rotten—bastard! I'll kill you...!'

Each time Guy fell to the ground, Henry pulled him up again and again. Guy Trent was senseless, could not even put up his arms to protect himself from the vicious onslaught, let alone put up any kind of defensive fight.

Finally exhausted, Henry let him fall to the ground and stood over him, swaying and panting. He aimed one last vicious kick into his victim's groin and then turned away and stumbled through the wood, back to the sanctuary of the village leaving Guy Trent bleeding and unconscious on the cold ground.

CHAPTER 10

They found him six hours later.

When Sir Matthew became aware that his son's horse had returned home riderless, he sent some of his own household to search.

They carried him home, more dead than alive, and Sir Matthew called in the apothecary.

'Well?' he demanded as the apothecary, William Dale, came into his study after attending to Guy Trent's injuries. He was a portly, middle-aged man, with a hearty manner.

'A-hem, well now, it seems to me that the young man's injuries have not been caused by a mere fall from his horse. Oh dear me, no! They have been *inflicted* by some person or persons—I am convinced of it.'

William Dale sipped the brandy the footman handed him and watched Sir Matthew Trent's face darken.

'Some brawl, I suppose,' Sir Matthew muttered and sighed. 'The young devil's always in some scrape or another.'

'Possibly, possibly. Remarkably good brandy this, if I may say so. But if you want my opinion, Sir Matthew, *this* time it was not of your son's making.'

'What do you mean by that?'

The apothecary shrugged. 'It seems to me—and I've seen a good few of these cases, mark you...'

'Get on with it, man,' Sir Matthew rapped testily.

William Dale continued in his own time, not in the least daunted by Sir Matthew. The power he wielded in this neighbourhood as employer and magistrate did not intimidate William Dale, who regarded himself as a professional man, safe in the knowledge that there was no other physician for miles around with his expertise. No—he had naught to fear from Sir Matthew's temper. But those who had harmed his son would be in grave danger.

'To my mind,' he continued, sipping the brandy between phrases with irritating slowness. 'To my mind, your son has been set upon. Perhaps by thieves—or perhaps by someone who bears him a grudge.'

'What makes you think that?' Sir Matthew growled menacingly.

'Your son does not appear to have defended himself. He was too drunk for one thing,' he added baldly. 'There are no lacerations or bruises on his hands.' He doubled his fist and punched the empty air to demonstrate. 'See what I mean? In an equal fight there would be such evidence—and also I would expect to see bruising on his forearms where he'd put up his arms to protect himself. Where d'you say he was found?'

'In the wood on the road to Amberly.'

'And his horse returned home riderless?'

'Yes, yes.'

'Hmmm. Seems to me,' the apothecary

mused shrewdly. 'He—or they—lay in wait for him in the woods. Probably frightened his horse and it threw him. Then they set upon your son.' He finished the brandy with a flourish and got to his feet.

Sir Matthew put up his hand, palm outwards. 'Just a minute. What *exactly* are my son's injuries?'

'A broken nose, severe bruising to all areas of his face, particularly his eyes. Two teeth broken, a cut lower lip and a damaged ear. He'll probably be deaf in one ear for the rest of his life. Add to that severe bruising in the groin and the risk of a severe chill since we must presume he lay in the open for most of the night.'

'I—see.'

'I'll call again tomorrow, Sir Matthew. Good-day to you.'

'Good-day,' Sir Matthew murmured automatically, but already his thoughts were elsewhere.

He knew who had attacked his son and that man would be made to suffer for it.

Not for nothing had Sir Matthew become magistrate for this district. It gave him not only power over the villagers as their employer, it gave him absolute power over every aspect of their lives!

Ironically, it fell to Thomas Cole to arrest the man Sir Matthew believed had attacked his son.

Sir Matthew had consulted Lord Royston who was also a magistrate and considered senior to Sir Matthew by way of position, wealth and power.

'I want this man arrested and tried for attempted murder,' Sir Matthew had told him bluntly.

Lord Royston had sighed and waved his hand towards Sir Matthew in a gesture of dismissal. 'Do whatever you have to, Trent. It's no concern of mine. I've got my own problems,' he muttered.

Thomas Cole knocked at the door of the low, squat cottage. It was opened by Beth Miller, who, with no premonition of the disaster which was about to fall upon her family, politely invited the bailiff to step inside.

Joseph Miller, who had not been able to find casual work that week, was at home. He rose from his chair at the table. Mrs Miller looked up but did not rise. Ella continued to eat her meal without noticing Thomas Cole.

Of Sarah there was no sign.

'Is there something wrong, mister?'

'I'm afraid so, Miller,' Thomas Cole sighed. He had no stomach for the task he had to do. He had not wanted the job of parish constable along with that of bailiff on the estate, but he had been desperate for employment not too far from his parents in Amberly and, knowing Abbeyford to be in the main a law-abiding community, he had agreed.

Now he regretted becoming keeper of the peace.

'Joseph Miller—I am instructed by Sir Matthew Trent as magistrate of this parish to arrest you on a charge of attempted murder of his son, Guy Trent.'

Ellen Miller screamed. Joseph's mouth gagged open and he sat down heavily in his chair as if his legs had given way beneath him. Beth's sharp eyes darted from her father's stricken face to Thomas Cole.

'It weren't me pa, it were Hen...'

'Hold your tongue, girl!' Joseph Miller snapped, recovering his senses swiftly. Slowly he rose again from his seat at the table. Bemusedly he looked around the small, dingy room, as if feeling this might be the last time he saw it.

'You'll come peaceable-like?' Thomas Cole asked.

'Aye, I'll give you no trouble, mister. Seems as if I'm in enough already!'

Ellen's customary composure deserted her. She fell to her knees and clasped her husband about the legs. 'Joseph—tell him! Tell him it weren't you. Tell him the truth!'

Joseph Miller bent down towards his wife. 'Hush, woman. It's better this way. Think on Sarah.'

Still Ellen clung to her man. 'Sarah! Sarah!' Her voice rose to hysterical pitch. 'Why must you always think of her? After what she's done? She's the cause of all this. All these years we've been an honest, hard-working family with naught to fear from the justices. And now—now...' She choked on the words, could not speak of the fear that was in her heart.

Justice, metered out by the squire or the lord, was swift and severe. If Joseph Miller walked out of their cottage now, Ellen knew she might never more see him back there!

At best it would be prison, at worst swinging from the gibbet!

Gently Joseph released himself from her clinging, careworn hands, stood and squared his shoulders. His face was ashen, but his voice was steady as he said, 'I am ready to come wi' you, mister.'

As they left the cottage, Henry Smithson met them. He stopped, his eyes glancing from one to the other as they passed him.

From the doorway Beth shouted. 'He's takin' our pa, Henry Smithson, for summat you done!'

Thomas Cole hesitated, stopped and turned round. Joseph stopped but did not turn about.

'Is that true, Miller?'

'You 'ad orders to arrest *me*, didn't you, mister?' Joseph muttered, looking steadfastly ahead.

'Yes, but...'

'Then you're arresting me.'

Once more Thomas Cole looked towards Henry Smithson, standing there, not moving, saying nothing.

'It's a bad business,' Thomas murmured, 'a bad business.' And, turning, took hold of Joseph Miller's arm and made to lead him away.

Then Joseph did look back, his dark eyes boring into Henry. 'Look to our Sarah, lad. You know what you mun do, dun't you?' The two men stared at each other, then slowly Henry nodded.

Satisfied, Joseph turned and walked away without a backward glance.

In the attic bedroom beneath the thatch Beth leant over her sister lying on the bed.

'Do you hear, the bailiff's taken Pa—accused of murder, he is? All because of you.'

Sarah's violet eyes flew open and the last vestige of colour in her already pale and sickly face drained away.

'Pa? Oh no! Why do they think it were Pa?'

Beth smiled wryly. 'They knows Pa has no love for the Trents an' because of *you* they think he done for Master Guy.'

Sarah struggled to sit up. 'Guy—he—he's not dead?'

Beth screeched and lashed out at her sister, the palm of her hand striking Sarah's cheek. 'You still think of *him*— even now.

Think on Pa! What'll they do to Pa? They'll likely *hang* him!'

At eight o'clock on an early September morning in the year of 1796 Sarah Miller married Henry Smithson. No one attended the ceremony except the Reverend Hugh Langley and sufficient persons to witness the ceremony legally.

They married because Joseph Miller demanded it. Sarah, because he was her father and there was no other way to cover the shame of her swelling belly, and Henry Smithson agreed because Joseph Miller stood accused of the crime he, Henry, had committed. In tacit agreement made in those few moments when Thomas Cole arrested Joseph Miller, Henry had understood what was expected of him.

Joseph would keep silent if Henry would marry Sarah and take her bastard as his own.

Grimly Henry walked beside Sarah from the church back to the Millers' cottage where he would now live with his bride.

Once he had loved this girl in his own rough way, but his heart was filled with hatred—against Guy Trent, even against Joseph Miller for forcing him into a position where he was obliged to marry Sarah when she had belonged to another man. And most of all he hated Sarah for betraying the love he had had for her, for giving herself to young Trent, for lying with him, for...

Each time he thought of them together he felt the violence creep over him again and knew that though they had to spend the rest of their lives together, he would never forgive and never forget!

They entered the Millers' cottage. Ellen Miller sat in front of the cold hearth, her hands lying idle in her lap, her eyes staring and vacant. Ella in her corner rocked to and fro, clutching her rag-doll close to her thin chest.

Beth was tying a shawl about her head.

'Seems I mun become milkmaid now,' she greeted them resentfully, 'else we shall all starve.'

'Is there any news?' Henry asked, whilst Sarah lowered herself into a chair opposite her mother and bowed her head.

Beth's eyes met Henry's. 'But for you Henry Smithson, he'd be here where he belongs, not standing 'afore the magistrate.'

Roughly Henry grasped Beth's arm and

twisted it cruelly. 'I'll not take that from you or anyone else. Your father knows what he is about.'

Beth glanced at Sarah. 'Aye, an' so do we all. He's sacrificing himsel' for *that!'* She flung her arm out in a gesture towards Sarah.

'An' he's not the only one, an' don't you forget it,' Henry said grimly.

They stood staring at each other, the man with bitterness in his heart, the girl with her badly pock-marked face, full of resentment. Then Beth shook herself free of his grasp and left the cottage. Ellen Miller had not stirred, had not seemed to notice the heated exchange of conversation. She continued to stare into space.

'Well, Sarah Smithson. You'd best start being a wife. Seems your ma has given up. I'll be away to me work.'

As the cottage door banged behind her husband, Sarah covered her face and wept, the sobs racked her body. But no comforting hands reached out to her. Guy's embrace was lost to her for ever, and even her mother, who sat only a few feet from her, did not reach out to comfort her conscience-stricken daughter.

CHAPTER 11

Joseph Miller squared his shoulders and faced Sir Matthew across the wide expanse of the leather-topped desk in Sir Matthew's study at the Manor.

As local magistrate, Sir Matthew was entitled to hold the 'court' at his home.

Thomas Cole cleared his throat and attempted, from his scant knowledge of such proceedings, to carry out his duties correctly.

'Joseph Miller, you are hereby charged that on the night of August thirtieth last you did wilfully assault Mister Guy Trent with the premeditated intention of causing him fatal injury. How do you plead? Guilty or not guilty?'

There was silence in the room whilst Sir Matthew and Thomas Cole waited for the accused man to reply. Joseph fixed his gaze upon the window behind Sir Matthew's chair, clamped his jaw firmly shut and said nothing.

'Well, man, speak up, did you do it or

didn't you?' Sir Matthew Trent thundered.

Still Joseph did not speak.

Thomas Cole sighed heavily. He didn't like all this. Not one bit. Ever since the moment he had arrested Joseph Miller he had doubted that the man accused had had anything at all to do with the attack on young Trent. And now the fool refused to speak in his own defence.

'Sir Matthew,' Thomas Cole murmured. 'I think Miller is protecting someone, I think...'

'Nonsense. If he won't speak up, then his silence must be taken as an admission of guilt. Well, Miller, have you naught to say?'

Joseph continued to stare steadfastly above Sir Matthew's head.

Sir Matthew viewed the accused man standing before him through narrowed eyes. He knew he had to be careful. He would have liked to have rid himself of Joseph Miller for ever, to have seen him at the end of a rope or at least transported to Botany Bay, but to turn the charge into a capital offence would mean the trial would have to be held in a higher court—and then he could not be sure that Miller would be found guilty, particularly if the whole sorry story of Guy's involvement with Miller's daughter—of the bastard she would bear him—were to come out.

Sir Matthew shuddered. He could not afford the scandal. No, he would keep the whole matter within his own power—especially since he had so far had the luck that Lord Royston did not wish to be involved.

He decided to pretend leniency.

'Now look here, Miller—in view of the unfortunate—er—circumstances concerning your daughter, which we both know about...'

Joseph's face remained impassive.

'...and because you didn't use a weapon on my son—only your own murderous fists...' Sir Matthew clenched his own fist in an attempt to hold his own temper in check. '...I am prepared to change the charge to a "common law misdemeanour" with a maximum sentence of two years' imprisonment with hard labour...'

Joseph gave no sign, but Sir Matthew heard Thomas Cole's shocked, swift intake of breath, but he ignored it.

'...and when you return to Abbeyford, I hope you will have learnt your lesson and...'

Thomas Cole was leaning across the desk, anger blazing in his usually docile eyes. 'Why, man, it's a death sentence you're giving him. In those gaols...'

'Nonsense, Cole. What would you prefer? To see him on the end of a gibbet?'

'It might be kinder...'

'It's not within my power to try a capital offence, he'd have to be tried in a higher court.'

'Well, let him be. Yes, let him. He might stand a better chance...'

'No!' Sir Matthew snapped. 'No—we'll deal with this ourselves.'

'I don't see anyone else present—only you!' Thomas Cole muttered. In desperation, he turned to Joseph. 'For God's sake man, speak out. *Did* you do it?'

He felt this was all wrong. Sir Matthew was using his power to rid himself of a troublesome element in the valley. Thomas Cole believed Miller innocent, but at least, even if guilty, the man should have had a proper court trial, with jury and a properly conducted hearing. This way, Sir Matthew was using his power—to Thomas's mind—unjustly.

Thomas groaned deep within himself.

Joseph Miller remained stubbornly silent.

Thomas turned back to Sir Matthew, rage bubbling up inside him. 'You can't *do* this—it's wrong!'

Sir Matthew glowered at him and said in a dangerously controlled voice, 'And why not, pray? Am I not squire and magistrate of this valley?'

'Aye, and I'm beginning to see why? You have no proof of this man's guilt and I tell you I have strong suspicions that he's definitely *not* the man! And yet you still send him to his death...'

Sir Matthew attempted to laugh. 'Imprisonment is not death.'

'Oh yes it is, and you well know it!' Thomas Cole thundered. '*If* he survives the hard labour, *if* he survives amongst the criminals and rogues he must live with, you know as well as I do that the gaol-fever will get him. You know all that and yet you still send him—I say—to his death.'

'I'll have no trouble-makers in my valley,' Sir Matthew growled. 'I still hold him responsible for those damaged fences.'

'But you've no *proof*—either about that or this attack on your son. You're just using this as an excuse to get rid of someone who has dared to stand up to you. A man who was only trying to protect his livelihood and his family. You reckon you can rob a man of his land, use his young lass for your pleasure and still expect him to touch his forelock to you. You're a dictator—a bloody murderer!'

Sir Matthew was on his feet. 'How *dare* you speak to me like that? Take care I don't dismiss you...'

'I'll not give you the chance. I won't work for you a minute longer!' Thomas Cole shouted.

For the first time Joseph Miller opened his mouth. 'Nay, Mister Cole, I don't hold you to blame for a' this. I wouldn't want you to lose your job 'cos 'o me.'

Thomas swung round, his soft brown eyes now blazing with indignant fury. 'Miller—why don't you speak up, man?' he demanded again.

With quiet resignation, Joseph said, 'I have me reasons, mister.'

'Aye, an' they must be good ones. Man, you're throwing your *life* away!'

Stubbornly, Joseph Miller's jaw hardened and he remained silent.

Thomas Cole's shoulders sagged in

defeat. 'I can do no more if you won't defend yoursel'.'

His eyes met the cold, hard stare of Sir Matthew Trent. He made one last desperate effort. 'What of his family? Will they be turned out of his cottage to starve?'

'No. If I understand things correctly,' Sir Matthew looked towards Joseph for denial. 'Your daughter is by this time married to young Smithson and he will move into your cottage? Is that correct?'

Joseph Miller's eyes came at last to rest upon Sir Matthew's gaze. For a long moment they glared at each other, a challenge of strong wills between the man who knew himself master and victor and the underling who knew himself beaten, yet still could not deny the pride in his blood.

Released from the necessity for silence, the flood of passion poured from Joseph's lips. 'Aye, they'll be wed by now. Your son's bastard will bear the name of Smithson.' He pointed his finger at Sir Matthew, 'And he'll be raised to bring revenge to you and yours for this day's work...'

'That's enough, Miller. Get him out of here, Cole.'

'No—I'll play no more part in this,' Thomas said doggedly.

Sir Matthew glared at him but Thomas Cole—so quiet, so gentle—had never felt such a violent anger against any human being until this moment. Nor was he going to let the matter rest there. He took a deep breath and said, 'I'll see Lord Royston...'

Sir Matthew gave a wry laugh. 'I doubt you'll be welcome there, Cole.'

Thomas Cole reddened. 'You'll find no one in this valley will lay a hand against Miller to help you put him in gaol.'

Sir Matthew smiled and said quietly, 'I had already foreseen that possibility.'

He moved and pulled the bell-cord. Instantly there was the sound of shuffling and rattling outside and the door flew open to reveal four tough, evil-looking men, completely unknown to either Thomas Cole or Joseph Miller.

'There's always those who'll undertake *any* kind of work, Cole, for a guinea or two,' Sir Matthew said smoothly.

Helplessly Thomas watched whilst the four men made to take hold of Joseph Miller and bear him away. Now he realised fully just how deep was Sir Matthew's hatred—and fear—of Joseph Miller.

As the men half-dragged Joseph from the room, he turned and now looked Sir Matthew full in the face, his final threat echoing in Sir Matthew Trent's ears.

'Tha'll rue the day your son defiled my girl, my Sarah... There'll be a curse upon the Trents! A curse...!'

'You can't come in here, my man,' the butler said loftily.

'I can—and I will!' Thomas Cole shouldered aside the butler and stepped into the spacious hall of Abbeyford Grange.

He paused a moment. Anger and a sense of outrage had brought him this far and would still carry him to face Lord Royston—but for the moment he paused, conscious of the fact that he was standing in Caroline's home.

As if his longing had transmitted itself to her, miraculously she appeared at the top of the wide, sweeping staircase.

'Thomas!' she breathed his name and started down the stairs towards him but at that moment the double doors to the morning-room were thrown open and Lord Royston appeared.

His surprise at seeing the estate's bailiff

standing there swiftly turned to anger as he saw Caroline hovering on the stairs. The impudence of the man! Daring to come here! He was about to open his mouth to speak, but Thomas Cole turned and completely ignoring Caroline strode purposefully towards him.

'I must speak with you on a very urgent matter, my lord.'

Misunderstanding, the earl said stiffly, 'I do not think there is anything we have to say to each other, Cole.'

Ignoring his dismissive air, Thomas persisted, 'My lord, please hear me out. There has been a serious miscarriage of justice. Sir Matthew Trent has sentenced Joseph Miller to two years imprisonment with hard labour for an alleged attack upon his son. I believe the man to be innocent.'

Lord Royston's eyes were hard, his mouth a thin line. Slowly, with deliberate emphasis, he said, 'I would trust Sir Matthew's judgement rather than yours. Whatever action he has taken has my full approval.'

Thomas Cole stared at him in disbelief. He had known the Earl of Royston to be a hard man, but had always believed him to be just. Now it seemed that Lord Royston could be as corrupt as Sir Matthew. His next words confirmed that he too would use this situation to bring about something he wanted. 'And since you have ranged yourself on the side of this villain I think you had better leave this district without delay, Cole, *without delay!*'

Thomas heard Caroline's cry of despair, but he did not look up. Instead he faced her father, fearless now, his resolution firm. 'And gladly, *my lord,*' he said with heavy sarcasm. 'Perhaps the Americas will treat a man more justly.'

He turned and walked towards the door.

'Thomas, oh Thomas!'

He heard her cry, but he neither looked back nor even hesitated.

The door closed behind him to the sound of Caroline's distraught weeping.

For Caroline, help came unexpectedly.

Lady Lynwood and her son paid a visit to the Grange and, whilst the old friends talked together, eagerly Caroline suggested that she and young Lynwood should go riding.

Lynwood noticed Lord Royston's hesitation but could not guess at the reason for it.

'I'll take good care of her, my lord.'

The earl's expression softened. The young boy, in his adoration of Caroline, could know nothing of the doubt in the older man's heart.

It was five days since Thomas Cole's visit to the Grange, during which time Lord Royston had scarcely let Caroline out of his sight.

Surely Cole would be gone by now? Surely he would not have dared to linger in Abbeyford?

'Very well then, but be back here before dusk.'

Gleefully Caroline ran to change into her riding-habit. 'Hilton, Hilton, have my horse saddled, will you? And bring Lord Lynwood's mount too.'

A short while later they were cantering down the grassy slope towards Abbeyford village.

Caroline reined in and breathed deeply at the fresh, clean air. 'Oh Francis, you don't know how good it is to be free, to get away from that house.'

Lynwood frowned, puzzled. 'I don't understand you.' He was disturbed to see that Caroline looked pale, with dark shadows beneath her eyes.

'Did you know that my father is arranging a marriage for me—to Lord Grosmore?'

The boy's face coloured. 'No, no I didn't.'

Caroline grimaced. 'Well, he is.'

'You—you're not—pleased?'

'I most certainly am not! 'Gros' by name and gross by build. Ugh, he's fat and ugly, Francis.'

All the time she was speaking her worried eyes were searching the fields and hillsides. Francis could feel her agitation.

'But, surely, your father only wants your happiness?'

Caroline's pretty mouth pouted. 'It seems in our social sphere one marries suitably—it doesn't signify whether or not one loves—or even likes—one's husband.'

Lynwood burst out, 'How I wish I were older!'

Caroline smiled and leaned across to pat his arm. 'Oh Francis, how sweet you are! Things don't seem so bad whilst I have you to champion my cause.'

Together they rode down into the valley, over the bridge near the smithy. Here Caroline slowed her horse to walking pace and looked down at him anxiously.

'I fear Captain is lame, Francis. How fortunate we are near the smith! I think he had better take a look at him.'

Lynwood dismounted, tethered his own horse to the rail outside the forge and held up his arms for Caroline to dismount. She slid into his arms. For a moment the young boy held her in his embrace. Though he was some four years younger, he was already taller than Caroline.

Coyly Caroline tossed her head and laughed. 'My, Francis, I hadn't realised how tall you've grown.'

Reluctantly, he let his arms fall from about her waist, knowing that because of the years that separated them, because she would not wait for him to grow up, his love for her could never be returned.

She was moving away from him, calling to the smith. 'Smith, are you there?'

A tall, broad-shouldered man appeared, his face red from the heat. 'M'lady.' He touched his forelock.

'I fear my horse, Captain, is lame. Will you take a look?'

'Certainly, m'lady.' The man caught hold of the bridle and led him into the forge. 'Steady, boy, steady,' he murmured soothingly to the animal. 'Now, let's take a look at you.'

Lady Caroline and Lynwood followed the smith and stood watching. Caroline began to fidget. 'Oh Francis, the heat is too much. I must get a breath of air!'

He turned and would have accompanied her outside again, but Caroline laid her hand upon his arm and smiled her most winning smile. 'No, I shall be all right, you stay. The smith may need you to hold Captain's head.' She turned and walked away. Lynwood hesitated, wanting to follow her, to stay with her, but she had asked him to remain here...

Caroline walked swiftly away from the forge and along the lane until she came to the cottage where Thomas Cole lived. Her heart was thumping wildly and she glanced back frequently to be sure Lynwood had not followed her. If only Thomas had not gone!

She tapped on the door and waited anxious moments, biting her lip. The door opened and he was standing before her.

'Caroline!'

She held her fingers to her lips and stepped inside the cottage. 'Thomas, oh

Thomas, my love! I have only a few moments—Lynwood is at the smith's with my horse...'

As she stepped into his cottage and saw that the room was in a state of turmoil, packing-cases and trunks standing open, Caroline turned wide, frightened eyes upon him. 'Thomas—you really are going away!'

'I must, my dear. I can no longer stay here—you know that.' His mouth was tight, his eyes bright once more with remembered anger.

'Yes...' she whispered.

'The man—Miller—was innocent, Caroline, I'm certain of it. But Trent wanted to be rid of him because he was a disturbing influence amongst the villagers.'

Caroline's eyes filled with tears. 'And my father? He would not help, would he?'

Sadly Thomas shook his head. 'No. It grieves me to think ill of him, my love. But—he would not.' Thomas sighed. 'I think he too saw a chance to rid himself of *my* presence.'

Caroline bit her trembling lip and held out her hands to him. 'Oh Thomas, I was so afraid you would have gone already.'

For a moment they were silent, staring at each other, their love for each other flowing between them.

'Thomas—Thomas—take me with you,' she begged, desperate because he was leaving her.

His arms were about her fiercely, his lips against her hair. 'Aye, b'God, an' I will! I'll play them at their own game!'

Caroline did not understand the bitterness behind his words—all she knew, all she cared about, was that he would not go away without her.

He held her away from him, his strong hands gripping her shoulders, his brown eyes boring into hers.

This was a new Thomas Cole—a masterful, decisive Thomas Cole. 'We must talk, make plans. How can we meet?'

Eagerly she said, 'The waterfall—I could get away from Lynwood and meet you there soon. He's at the smith's with my horse. I pretended Captain had gone lame so I could slip along here. I *had* to see if you were still here—I was so afraid...'

'Yes, yes,' Thomas Cole kissed her swiftly. 'Go now—quickly...'

Lynwood was already leading her horse out as Caroline hurried back towards the forge.

'The smith could find nothing amiss, Caroline.'

She forced a bright smile. 'Perhaps I was wrong. Come, help me mount and we will continue our ride.'

They skirted the village and rode up through the pastures towards the abbey ruins.

Caroline's merry laugh came bouncing across the breeze to him. 'Come, Francis, I'll race you to the woods.'

She spurred her horse to a gallop and was away across the grass before Lynwood had realised what she was doing.

When he reached the edge of the wood, she had disappeared amongst the trees. He could neither see nor even hear her horse. Lynwood groaned. After his confident promise to Lord Royston to take care of her, he had lost her.

'Caroline, Caroline!' At walking pace he rode amongst the trees, following a track, then doubling back and trying a different direction. He came to the roadway leading to the Manor and followed it until he stood at the edge of the wood overlooking the valley. He scanned the hill slopes, the lanes and pastures. There was no sign of Caroline.

'Caroline, *Caroline!*' he called in desperation, his heart pumping fearfully. Through the wood again he continued northwards until he came to the road leading from Abbeyford through the trees to Amberly. There was no one on the road, no one to ask if they had seen her. All was silent and still save for the distant sounds of the waterfall. Ducking beneath the trees, Francis rode on towards it and felt relief flood through him as he saw Captain tethered near some bushes at the top of the cliff overhanging the fall. Then swiftly, he felt a stab of terror. Had she fallen? Was she lying injured below, or worse, in the pool?

'Caroline!'

Young Lynwood flung himself from his horse and ran to the edge of the cliff. He was about to scramble down the rough pathway when he stopped.

Below him, near the pool, oblivious to his presence, stood Caroline. With her was the Abbeyford estate bailiff—Thomas Cole—his arms around her, his lips against her neck.

Unobserved by either of the lovers, standing on the very edge of the sheer drop, Lynwood stood motionless. Transfixed, unable to leave, he watched them, the pain growing in his chest, the hurt that Caroline, so lovely, so pure, could be meeting someone in clandestine furtiveness. Now he realised the reason for Lord Royston's reluctance to allow Caroline to go riding that morning. And worse, Caroline had used him, Lynwood, to escape from her father's watchful eye and meet her lover. The use she had made of him, the deceit she had practised upon him, hurt almost more than seeing her in the arms of Thomas Cole. He had not wanted to believe ill of her, but now there was no escaping from the truth.

Young Lynwood turned from the edge of the cliff and retched upon the grass.

He had idolised Caroline, worshipped her as an untouchable goddess. But his goddess had fallen from the pedestal on which he had placed her and the boy suffered the first pain of total disillusionment and disappointed love.

In those few short moments the Earl of Lynwood grew to manhood.

CHAPTER 12

The village was stunned by the news of the sentence Joseph Miller received. Justice was swift and severe—they all knew and accepted this—but in Abbeyford very few people ever broke the law and only the very oldest inhabitant could remember the last hanging in the village and that had been for sheep-stealing by a young man desperate for food with a young and starving family after the Bill of Enclosure had taken his land and livelihood.

Sarah wept. It seemed as if these days her eyes were constantly red-rimmed. The rosiness was gone from her cheeks. As her body became swollen with child, her youthful bloom was lost for ever. Her black hair became lank and lifeless, her face puffed and blotchy. Wearily she dragged herself about the cottage, but the home that had once been warm and comforting was now a dismal and unhappy place.

Joseph Miller never saw his family again, for, just as Thomas Cole had predicted, seven weeks after his committal to prison, Joseph died of gaol-fever. From the day he was taken from his cottage, Ellen Miller had sat in a chair by the cold hearth, her eyes vacant, her hands idle. She neither spoke nor could she be persuaded to eat.

A week after the news of Joseph's death had reached them, she died in her sleep. Beth found her in the morning, the life gone out of her body as it had gone from her spirit the day her husband had been snatched from her.

Ella, who had depended solely upon her mother's care, pined, developed consumption and followed her mother to the grave in a few short weeks.

Beth wrapped her few belongings into a bundle and took the road out of Abbeyford, vowing never to set foot in the valley again.

'There's work to be had in the manufactories in Manchester and such cities for the likes o' me. Why, amongst them city girls, even *my* face won't be out o' place!'

Now there was only Henry Smithson and she in the cottage as Sarah came near the time to give birth to her child—Guy's child.

When Guy Trent had recovered sufficiently to leave his room, it was to find that things had changed vastly. Sarah—his lovely Sarah—was married to Henry Smithson and beyond his reach for ever.

Joseph Miller was gone from the village and the Miller family broken. Sir Matthew's tyrannical treatment of Miller had stirred resentment in each and every villager. Realising this, he planned steps to restore himself in the eyes of the simple village folk as their benevolent squire.

'Well, my boy, after this escapade, 'tis time you settled down and took yourself a wife. I have arranged a marriage between you and Louisa Marchant, the daughter of a clothing manufacturer near Manchester. He has promised a generous settlement upon his daughter...'

Guy Trent rode his horse like a maniac away from Abbeyford towards Manchester, his heart filled with fury. The marriage was fixed for November and all the village would be invited to attend a grand feast in the barn at the Manor to celebrate their master's son's wedding. In this way, Sir Matthew hoped to banish the bitter memories from the minds of his tenants and employees. He would feast them and entertain them and make them forget that he had ever been anything but the kindly, charitable master he fondly imagined they had always believed him to be.

On the very day of Guy's marriage to Louisa Marchant, in the cottage in the village Sarah Smithson gave birth to his child. Though two months premature, the boy survived. There was no rejoicing at the birth of Evan Smithson. In the pain of her labour, Sarah cried out for Guy. Her cries for her lover finally destroyed the last shreds of Henry's affection for Sarah. He would never forgive. He would never forget. Henry looked upon the bawling, red-haired babe with loathing and vowed to sow the seed of revenge within the child against his own sire!

'Papa, we are invited to Guy Trent's wedding,' Caroline had told her father some weeks before the proposed date. Lord Royston smiled tenderly upon her. For the past few weeks she had been good-humoured, obedient and a most loving daughter towards him.

He congratulated himself.

Thomas Cole was gone from Abbeyford—he had checked on that. And Lord Royston now presumed—indeed hoped—that the young man was already safely out of England bound for America.

As Lord Royston had confidently expected, Caroline seemed to have realised her foolishness when she had had more chance to observe the differences between Lord Grosmore—a man of unquestionable high birth and wealth—and Thomas Cole, the estate's bailiff.

Grosmore had become a constant visitor to the Grange and, though at first Caroline had been most ungracious towards her suitor, during the past few weeks Lord Royston had noticed a marked change in her attitude. She received Grosmore more kindly and seemed animated in his company.

Only the previous day Grosmore had sought out the earl and, with great pomposity, had asked for his daughter's hand in marriage. Royston had agreed at once, relieved that his strong-willed daughter would soon be safely married and out of danger from entering into any more such unsuitable liaisons. Royston shuddered and his thankfulness at the happy resolution to his worries made him say now, in a generous and expansive mood, 'No doubt Trent will organise entertainment for the villagers in his barn, but perhaps we should offer for them to hold the wedding reception and ball here—at the Grange. After all, Trent, and I believe Marchant too amongst *trade* circles, are both well thought of.'

'Why, Papa—that is an excellent idea.'

'And—er—would it not be an opportune moment to announce your own engagement to Lord Grosmore?'

Caroline hesitated and for a moment there was, deep in her green eyes, a flash of anger, of rebellion. Fear stabbed at Lord Royston. More sharply than he intended to speak to her, he said, 'I trust you do intend to accept him?'

For a moment a bleak, desolate expression flickered across her face. Then quietly Caroline said, 'It seems I have no choice.'

Inwardly Lord Royston sighed with relief. Outwardly he beamed once more upon his daughter. 'Good, good. You shall have a new ball-gown. And I have a surprise in store for you, my dear, but that is to be my own special secret.'

Caroline seemed to be lost in her own

thoughts and merely murmured some reply. Lord Royston patted her shoulder and smiled to himself.

No doubt it was quite usual for a young bride-to-be to be a little dreamy and distant, her thoughts already on the future life she would share with her wealthy, aristocratic husband.

It seemed the whole county attended Guy Trent's wedding—though that was not strictly accurate. Because of the Earl of Royston's involvement, the wedding was attended by many aristocratic people who would not normally have condescended to be present at the marriage of a squire's son to the daughter of a man in trade—wealthy though he may be!

The small village church was overflowing with guests and the Reverend Langley was flustered with the honour, the importance, the responsibility!

Guy Trent stood facing the altar as his bride entered the church on her father's arm. He neither turned to watch her walk towards him, nor even looked down to greet her as she stood uncertainly at his side.

It was the first of many heartaches Guy

Trent was to inflict upon the young girl. Louisa Marchant had come to Abbeyford as a young and attractive bride, full of hope and shy affection for her handsome, virile husband.

But her illusions, her hopes, were to be swiftly shattered, for Guy would never, could never, love Louisa when that love belonged for ever to Sarah.

Why he had ever loved—and would continue to long for—the black-haired, vivacious village girl, instead of the cool, serene, well-bred beauty of his wife, neither Guy Trent nor anyone else could ever explain.

Guy would spend the rest of his life in the Manor only a mile or so away from Sarah in her peasant's cottage and yet they were as lost to each other as if half the world separated them.

Louisa would shed many tears and, although Guy would do his duty as her husband and she would bear him a son, over the years her misery would grow into a cold bitterness.

But on this day of merry-making only Guy—and his Sarah alone in her labour giving birth to his son—could foresee what desolation the years ahead would hold.

The rest of the village caroused in the barn at the Manor, whilst their master's entertainment at the Grange was a little more refined.

After a sumptuous banquet Lord Royston rose to make the usual speech of good wishes to the bride and bridegroom and then added, 'And it is my happy duty to announce the engagement of my beloved daughter, Caroline, to Peter, Viscount Grosmore.'

There were cries of delight and surprise amongst the guests and Caroline found herself being gazed upon with fond eyes.

Only Lord Lynwood, seated beside his mother, turned ashen at Lord Royston's words and kept his eyes averted. He could not bear to see Caroline's unhappiness. Even though she had used and abused him, had destroyed his trust in her by her secret affair with Thomas Cole, which must now have been at an end, in spite of all that, Lynwood could not bear to think of her being obliged to marry a man she disliked, the odious, pompous, gross Grosmore!

When he did dare to look at her, Lynwood was surprised to see a faint smile upon her lips and calm acceptance in her eyes. He watched as Lord Grosmore, with a great fuss and flourish, placed the ring upon her finger—a huge ruby, far too large and gaudy for Caroline's slim fingers.

Then Lord Royston gave his daughter a silver locket set with a ruby surrounded by smaller diamonds. As he fastened the delicate chain around her neck and stooped to kiss his daughter's smooth brow, Caroline opened the locket and saw the two tiny miniature portraits of her dear mother and father. Lynwood saw her mouth quiver, her eyes fill with tears, saw her clasp her father's hand and hold it against her cheek for an instant. But then she was in control of her emotions once more, graciously receiving the congratulations and good wishes of those present with a gentle smile upon her lips. But Lynwood wondered...

He only had a chance to speak to her briefly as they danced.

'Caroline—are you—happy?'

Her eyes were shining, her lips parted. 'Oh yes, dear Francis—I am going to be so happy.'

As the dance ended she held both his hands in hers for a moment and looked up at him her green eyes beseeching him,

'Francis—you will always think well of me, won't you? You will always—understand?'

Thinking she was in some way asking for his forgiveness for her past foolishness, he answered, 'Of course, of course I will. Need you ask?'

She touched his cheek lightly with her fingertips. 'Dear Francis—don't ever forget me, will you?'

Then she was moving away from him across the crowded floor and slipping quietly behind a heavy brocade curtain and through a door.

Only Lynwood, whose eyes had followed her all evening whilst she had danced and curtsyed and smiled at her fiancé, saw her go. Perhaps she is fatigued, he thought, for even after Guy Trent and his bride had left the company the dancing had gone on and on and it was now well after midnight.

Tired himself of the noise, the music and laughter, Lynwood went out on to the terrace overlooking the rose-garden. It was a mild November night, the moon and stars amazingly bright in the dark sky. Lynwood leant against the balustrade in the shadows, listening to the muted strains of the music and thinking of Caroline.

He must have been there some time

when a small sound disturbed his thoughts.

He shrank further into the shadows as he saw a figure hidden by a dark cloak and hood glide along the terrace towards him. As she neared the steps only a few feet away from him, she paused and glanced back over her shoulder. For a moment the hood of her cloak fell back from her face and Lynwood recognised her.

He almost cried her name aloud: *'Caroline!'* but no sound came from his lips.

He saw her falter, saw her fingers touch the locket at her throat, saw her glance back towards the lighted windows where her father's guests still danced away the night, where Lord Grosmore searched amongst the dancers for his fiancée.

In the bright moonlight, Lynwood fancied he saw a shudder pass through her slender frame, then she turned and, pulling the hood over her face once more, ran lightly down the stone steps into the rose-garden. Silently she flitted like an ethereal shadow along the twisting paths until she came to the door in the wall at the end of the garden which led into the field beyond.

As she slipped through it, Lynwood moved from his hiding-place and ran to the door. He reached it in time to see her running swiftly down the slope towards the footbridge.

From the shadow of the bushes beside the bridge, Lynwood could just discern the figure of a man emerge, saw him open his arms to her as she flew towards him and watched as she was enfolded into his loving embrace.

For a timeless moment the lovers clung together and then Thomas Cole lifted her on to one of the two horses tethered near the bushes.

As they rode away into the darkness, only Lynwood saw them go.

the door. He watched it in time to see her running swiftly down the slope towards the footbridge.

From the shadow of the bushes beside the bridge, Lynwood could just discern the figure of a man emerge, saw him open his arms to her as she flew towards him and watched as she was enfolded into his loving embrace.

For a timeless moment the lovers clung together and then Thomas Cole lifted her on to one of the two horses tethered near the bushes.

As they rode away into the darkness, only Lynwood saw them go.

This Large Print Book for the Partially sighted, who cannot read normal print, is published under the auspices of

THE ULVERSCROFT FOUNDATION

THE ULVERSCROFT FOUNDATION

. . . we hope that you have enjoyed this Large Print Book. Please think for a moment about those people who have worse eyesight problems than you . . . and are unable to even read or enjoy Large Print, without great difficulty.

You can help them by sending a donation, large or small to:

The Ulverscroft Foundation,
1, The Green, Bradgate Road,
Anstey, Leicestershire, LE7 7FU,
England.

or request a copy of our brochure for more details.

The Foundation will use all your help to assist those people who are handicapped by various sight problems and need special attention.

Thank you very much for your help.

Other MAGNA Romance Titles In Large Print

ROSE BOUCHERON
The Massinghams

VIRGINIA COFFMAN
The Royles

RUTH HAMILTON
Nest Of Sorrows

SHEILA JANSEN
Mary Maddison

NANCY LIVINGSTON
Never Were Such Times

GENEVIEVE LYONS
The Palucci Vendetta

MARY MINTON
Every Street